A Flair for Flip-Flops

A Flair for Flip-Flops

A Sadie Kramer Flair Mystery

DEBORAH GARNER

CRANBERRY COVE PRESS

*For all those who love mystery, flip-flops, and fun
in the sun — or any combination of the above.*

Books by Deborah Garner

The Paige MacKenzie Mystery Series

Above the Bridge
The Moonglow Café
Three Silver Doves
Hutchins Creek Cache
Crazy Fox Ranch

The Moonglow Christmas Novella Series

Mistletoe at Moonglow
Silver Bells at Moonglow
Gingerbread at Moonglow
Nutcracker Sweets at Moonglow
Snowfall at Moonglow

The Sadie Kramer Flair Series

A Flair for Chardonnay
A Flair for Drama
A Flair for Beignets
A Flair for Truffles
A Flair for Flip-Flops

Cranberry Bluff

ONE

Sadie kicked both feet out in front of her beach chair and admired her new pedicure. It just wouldn't have been right to go on a seaside vacation without a few stylish touches. She'd asked the lovely young girl at her favorite day spa to apply a light sky blue for the base color. With a tiny seashell design added on one of her big toes and a bright yellow sun on the other, it was perfect.

Nabbing the last available room at luxurious Casa Playa, a popular hideaway along the Southern California coast, had been a fortunate score. The boutique hotel's pet-friendly private beach right outside her room's sliding glass doors made it an ideal escape for Sadie and her favorite sidekick.

"What do you think, Coco?" Sadie looked down at the petite Yorkie, who was soaking up the warm sun. "I just love your beach towel. It's so great we found one just your size!" Okay, so it was a kitchen towel they'd found at a souvenir shop along the boardwalk, Sadie reminded herself. The nautical design fit the theme of their surroundings, and the towel itself helped keep sand out of Coco's fur.

Sadie tugged at the skirt on her one-piece bathing suit. She'd gotten over modesty a good decade ago, accepting her plump figure along with the inevitable slide from being middle-aged toward the golden years. But she still liked to be presentable. Besides, the exotic floral print picked up the recent highlights in her hair: red streaks mixed into her natural gray. She could hardly wait to drape her favorite red Peruvian beads over a new black tunic she'd picked up for that evening's event. It would be a stunning look for her new hair coloring.

Leaning back to soak up the sun, she smiled at the timing of her visit. She'd been unaware of the private celebrity events when she'd made the hotel reservation, not to mention her surprise when the hotel clerk handed her invitations with her hotel key. Common sense told her it was a mistake. She hardly ran with a Hollywood crowd, and it was unlikely the hotel was including all guests in the festivities. But she'd never been one to pass up an adventure, whether planned or not. The thought of a celebrity dinner followed by a cast party a few days later was simply too enticing to turn down. She'd politely taken the check-in packet with a smile.

Sadie never followed the tabloids, but she certainly knew who Garrison Quinlan was. How could she not? His face beamed from the cover of nearly every magazine, whether *People, Rolling Stone*, or *Time*. To say he'd graced the cover of *GQ* multiple times went without saying, considering his initials. Had the magazine not been founded long before he was born, the general public might have considered it named after him. Some of his younger fans likely did anyway.

Garrison Quinlan's type had never appealed to Sadie. True, he was a looker, handsome to a fault. She couldn't deny that; there was nothing wrong with her eyesight. But he was also flashy, fake-tanned, and full of himself. His signature move of starting every personal appearance with the shout "Do you love me?" seemed a tad over the top. Of course, screams and proclamations of adoration followed every time. He'd then reward his fans with a gleaming smile of perfectly aligned pearly whites, which only turned up the volume.

"It's not the same thing," Sadie said aloud, thinking back to her early years. She looked down at Coco, who opened one sleepy eye questioningly. "The Beatles never *asked* us to scream. It was simply a basic reflex. Not the same thing at all."

In spite of her own personal lack of GQ fan fever, the occasions promised to be entertaining. No doubt the people-watching aspect would be intriguing as well.

"That's enough sun for today." Sadie stood, tossed her towel over her shoulder, and folded her beach chair into a compact bundle of cloth and metal.

Coco, seeing Sadie stand, hopped up and gathered the kitchen towel in her teeth, ready to follow her favorite human wherever she headed.

"I'll carry that for you, Coco. I don't want you to trip." Coco, always on the lookout for a game of tug-of-war, held on briefly to the edge of the terrycloth material before surrendering and letting go. "Thank you," Sadie said. She tossed Coco's towel over her own and patted the Yorkie on the head.

The hotel room was cool as Sadie stepped inside and closed the sliding glass doors, certainly refreshing after being outside in the sun. The seaside décor added to the soothing feeling. Pale blue walls, light wood furniture, and soft watercolor prints of beach scenes blended together to create a calming environment. If not for the event that evening, Sadie would have been tempted to throw on capris and a T-shirt and read until she fell asleep. Instead, she splashed cold water on her face and made a phone call.

"Flair! Good afternoon!" Amber's voice was full of pep, as always. Sadie smiled, grateful for the energetic young lady on the other end of the line. Her San Francisco fashion boutique, Flair, always ran well under Amber's management. Sadie knew she was fortunate to have Amber in charge of the shop. Many businesses had problems when owners were away.

"How's everything going?" Sadie leaned back in a blue-and-white-striped armchair, pleased to feel the soft cushioning against her back.

"It's been fairly quiet," Amber said. "We've had a few customers, but mostly downtime. I've been restocking the summer racks, making sure we have all sizes out. I have a list going of things we might want to order, like more sparkly sunglasses."

"Oh, good idea," Sadie said, remembering she'd brought a pair with her. She and Amber had found the glittery sunglasses at a recent trade show and ordered them in every color. The one currently in her suitcase was purple, which reminded her she needed something to wear it with. A shopping excursion on the beach boardwalk was in order.

"How's everything going with your vacation so far?" Amber asked. "Nice room? Good scenery?"

"Wonderful room and excellent scenery," Sadie said. "I have an ocean view, and the sand comes right up to a private patio area outside the back doors. There's a small kitchenette too. I could hide away in here for the whole week if I wanted to."

"You should," Amber said. "Curl up with some good mystery books and call room service when you need something. That beach patio sounds like heaven. You can just relax and enjoy the privacy. Aside from the shopping excursions you'll undoubtedly take, that is."

Sadie laughed. Amber knew her well. She wasn't about to pass up the opportunity to browse the local beach shops. "That's my basic plan except for an event tonight that came up unexpectedly, as well as one later in the week."

"What kind of events?" Amber asked. "Now you have my

curiosity up. You do seem to stumble into unusual gatherings. Maybe another winery festival? Or a theater production?" Amber rattled off a few other guesses.

"None of the above," Sadie said. "But both should be interesting, and it seems I've sort of been invited to them."

"How can you sort of be invited to something?" Amber's tone held a hint of laughter.

"Apparently, easily," Sadie said. "There were invitations in my check-in packet, right between my room key and a hotel property map. I suspect it might have been a mistake, but…" Her voice trailed off. Why turn down opportunities for good meals and entertainment?

"Those must be guest receptions," Amber said. Sadie could hear her clicking hangers on racks. "Some upscale hotels do that. You know, wine and cheese, managers saying hello, that type of thing."

"This is a bit more than that," Sadie said. "These are celebrity functions for…" She lowered her voice even though it seemed ridiculous. No one could hear her except Coco. "For Garrison Quinlan."

"*What?*" Amber shrieked, almost causing Sadie to drop her phone. "For GQ? I *love* him!"

Sadie sighed. Of course Amber loved him. Everyone loved him.

"Take me with you!" Amber squealed.

"That might be difficult," Sadie pointed out. "The first one is in four hours, and you're a solid eight hours away." She lifted Coco into her lap and scratched the spot between her ears. Coco exhaled a sigh of contentment.

"Minor details," Amber muttered, then sighed. "I'll just have to live vicariously through you."

"I'll make sure to enjoy it for you," Sadie offered.

———

"And when he asks if you love him, you have to say *yes*," Amber said.

Sadie laughed. "How about if I just say 'Amber loves you.'" She could hear Amber clapping her hands in approval.

"Even better," Amber said.

"Speaking of love," Sadie prompted, "should I also say Dylan loves him?" Amber had been dating Dylan for several months, a detail she seemed to have forgotten during the conversation.

"Er… maybe not," Amber said, laughing. "He thinks GQ is shallow."

"I knew I trusted Dylan's judgment," Sadie said.

A chime on the other end of the phone call signaled a customer entering the shop. Saying a quick goodbye, she let Amber go attend to business. She set Coco down in the portable travel "palace" they always took on trips but left the door open so the petite canine could wander in and out. Considering the silk and velvet interior of the custom-built kennel, it came as no surprise when Coco curled up, placed her head on her paws, and closed her eyes.

"That's right, Coco," Sadie said. "Get some beauty sleep. I suspect we have an interesting evening ahead of us."

Yes. It should be quite an evening indeed.

TWO

Sadie looked at the directory elegantly encased in glass on the lobby wall. Three event rooms were listed: Gran Sala del Mar, Gran Sala del Cielo, and Gran Sala de las Estrellas. Living in California, Spanish names weren't unfamiliar, and her language abilities were enough to recognize the three grand rooms named after the sea, the sky, and the stars, respectively. It seemed fitting that the event for Garrison Quinlan would be held in the Gran Sala de las Estrellas. After all, he was a star of superstardom stature.

Having had no idea she'd be attending the event, Sadie was pleased to see the spacious room boasted a theme of black, white, and red. She couldn't have planned a better outfit if she tried. The white linen tablecloths on the round banquet tables would look formal against her black tunic, not to mention their resemblance to her silver hair. Folded black napkins in the shape of swans looked elegant, albeit a touch foreboding in a *Swan Lake* sort of way. And the bold centerpieces of red carnations and roses picked up the streaked highlights in her hair as well as her red Peruvian beads. All in all, she blended in nicely with the décor. She found this comforting—especially since she didn't expect to know a single person there. At least she looked like she belonged.

Seeing only a few people, Sadie wondered if she'd committed an etiquette faux pas. "Apparently, we missed the memo about being fashionably late," she whispered to her tote bag, which was casually slung over her arm. A soft yip came from inside, where Coco curled up on a velvet pillow, as she always did when Sadie was on the go. The basic tote hardly matched Sadie's outfit, but it wouldn't matter once she placed it on the floor next to her chair. Which reminded her… where was she supposed to sit?

A casual stroll through the room quickly told her she would *not* be sitting at any of the front tables. Name cards in swirling calligraphy dotted each place setting of the first… and second… and third… all in all, four rows of tables. The fifth and sixth rows didn't have specific names at each place, but folded cardboard tents with the word Reserved stood propped up on each seat. By the time she reached the seventh row of tables, she had already resigned herself to sitting in the back. She continued to the eighth and last row and took a place near a side door. The only way she could possibly be farther away would be to step outside altogether. That was fine, as far as she was concerned. She wasn't there as a participant but just as an observer—and for the free food, of course.

Sadie settled into the banquet chair and found a spot on the floor for her tote bag. She whispered a few cautionary words about proper manners at such an event, letting them drift downward. Although she'd had the foresight to add a tiny black-and-red bow to a topknot of fur on Coco's head, she knew it would be best if they both kept in control. That meant Sadie in her seat and Coco in the tote.

More guests arrived and then a few more until the room began to buzz with the excitement of a crowd dressed to impress and chattering for acceptance. A waiter stopped by Sadie's table to offer her one of a dozen flutes of champagne, all sparkling from their balanced positions on his tray. She accepted, took a sip, and set the glass down on the linen tablecloth with what she hoped was a Hollywood-worthy flourish. A trio of musicians launched into a medley of show tunes aimed to cover a wide gamut of musical tastes. Sadie tapped her foot to the music, her head tilting side to side along with each beat.

"Excuse me, is this seat taken?"

Sadie turned toward the voice, finding a middle-aged woman wearing a plum evening gown with chiffon sleeves that gathered loosely at her wrists. Her earrings—rhinestones, not diamonds, Sadie was certain—sparkled under the overhead lights. Her skin bore more wrinkles than expected for her apparent age, a sign of too many days soaking up the sun's rays, but her smile was warm and friendly. "Please," Sadie said, gesturing with one hand. "Be my guest."

"Thank you." The woman slid into the seat and set a silver clutch purse on the table. She extended a hand toward Sadie. "My name's Myrtle," she said.

Sadie responded with her own name as the waiter with the champagne passed by again, offering Myrtle a drink. A second waiter stopped by with a tray of miniature smoked salmon puff pastries. Myrtle and Sadie each took one, and a heavyset man approaching the table grabbed two before abruptly pulling out a chair and taking a seat across from them. He snapped his fingers to call the waiter with the champagne back to the table. Sadie and Myrtle exchanged looks as if the sudden intrusion bonded the two women as longtime friends. Whether the man intended to introduce himself or not, they wouldn't know since he was quickly joined by two others.

"Buddy, it's great to see you!" A stout, red-faced guy slapped the first man on the back and plopped into a chair beside him.

"Jack Davis!" Buddy exclaimed. "My, they let anyone in here don't they?"

"Always the joker, Buddy," Jack said. "You remember Marvin, don't you? From the last premiere?" He nodded toward a third man, a wiry fellow with a mop of hair that struck Sadie as a toupee. At least she hoped for the poor man's sake that it was.

"Of course." Buddy stuffed the second puff pastry in his mouth, brushed his hands against each other, and extended his arm to greet Marvin. "Buddy Barker. Good to see you again. I didn't realize you knew Jack," he said.

"Oh, Marvin and I go way back," Jack said. "Worked a lot together." He drummed his palms on the table. Sadie watched the champagne in her glass sway back and forth, and Myrtle steadied a spoon that was beginning to slide.

"It'll be great to see Garrison again," Buddy said. He unfolded a black linen swan and brushed a speck of puff pastry off his mouth.

"Absolutely," Jack replied. "I haven't seen him since that golf tournament at Torrey Pines." Marvin simply nodded, though Sadie wasn't sure if it was to agree that seeing Garrison would be good or that Marvin had also last seen him at the tournament.

"Very important men," Myrtle whispered, covering up her facetious comment with a cough.

"Indeed, they must be," Sadie whispered back. *Which is why they're at the very back table with us*, she added silently.

The musicians switched gears and headed into an up-tempo rendition of "There's No Business Like Show Business," which added to the energy level of the already-frenzied crowd. Some guests had taken places at tables, but many others still flitted around the room exchanging air kisses alongside one cheek and then the other.

As the song wound to an end, a tuxedo-clad gentleman

near the front of the hall tapped on a microphone, testing it. Assured that the sound system was in working order, he calmly said, "Welcome." The single word was enough to begin a flurry of movement as people flocked to their tables. After a slight pause, a second greeting of "Good evening" served to herd the rest of the attendees into their seats.

"You may not know me, but my name is James Chalinder." The man stepped back and smiled as a wave of laughter rolled through the crowd. Obviously, many already knew the man. Sadie hadn't the foggiest idea who he was. She glanced at Myrtle, who simply shrugged.

"I'm delighted to see you all here," the man continued, "as I'm sure Mr. Quinlan will be as well." A round of applause broke loose and then died down. "Our guest of honor will be arriving shortly, I'm sure. Meanwhile, I know you've all had a long day in the sun if you were wise enough to get here early—or a long day on the freeways if you weren't!" Another flurry of laughter followed. "So without further ado, let's get the delicious feast started now. Enjoy!"

On cue, multiple servers approached tables, setting a salad before each guest. Sadie looked at the mixture of greens as if being tested. *Arugula, radicchio, swiss chard, some type of sprout...* Not that it mattered. The candied pecans, dried cranberries, and feta cheese were enough to merit Sadie's approval. She took a bite and sighed with delight. The vinaigrette dressing was just sweet enough to bring out the flavor of the glazed nuts yet not overpowering. She and Myrtle exchanged looks of approval.

Silver trays of olive bread with ramekins of chive butter also landed on each table. Fortunately, a tray was placed on each side of the table, so Sadie and Myrtle were able to serve themselves without interfering in the boastful conversation among the three men across from them. The trio had yet to even say hello, which suited Sadie just fine. Being forward by nature, she normally would have jumped right in and introduced herself. But there was nothing appealing about these particular guests and quite a bit that was less than appealing. Content to enjoy the meal with the company of her new friend, Myrtle, Sadie buttered a piece of bread and let the server remove her empty salad plate.

James Chalinder, the man who had originally welcomed everyone—the emcee, Sadie assumed, still unsure who he was—had taken a seat at the first table, which was full other than one empty chair, presumably that of Garrison Quinlan. Fortunately, the scattering of chairs around each table just happened to allow a line of sight between Sadie and the front table. Over her slice of olive bread, Sadie noted Mr. Chalinder repeatedly checking his watch, as well as glancing at the empty place setting beside him. At one point he inserted a finger inside his collar and tugged at it slightly as if attempting to loosen its grip around his neck.

"That man looks uncomfortable, even worried," Sadie whispered to Myrtle, who followed Sadie's gaze to the front.

"He seemed relaxed enough when he welcomed everyone," Myrtle said, leaning closer to Sadie to observe from her viewpoint. She kept her voice low, as did Sadie, although Buddy, Marvin, and Jack had yet to even acknowledge their existence. "You're right," Myrtle continued. "He looks agitated now."

"Yes," Sadie said. "That's the perfect word for it: agitated. I wonder why."

"Something must not be going according to plan," Myrtle suggested. "I don't envy him. I despise being in charge of large events."

Sadie nodded. She'd coordinated important gatherings for her late husband's business. It always ended up being more stressful than enjoyable. Either the caterers forgot something, or the PA system malfunctioned, or the guest list was incomplete, or something else went wrong. It was rare for an event to run without a single hiccup when there were so many moving parts. With the celebrity aspect of this particular dinner, she could only imagine the pressure. Still, she found Mr. Chalinder's behavior curious.

Another round of plates glided onto the table. Distracted by the emcee's unease, Sadie regarded the miniature poultry set atop a sweet potato puree with caramelized onions, only half-attentive. Myrtle leaned closer and whispered, "Cornish game hen."

"Oh, yes," Sadie said, snapping out of her reverie. "So I see. Wonderful." Coco was going to love this if she could figure a sly way of dropping a few bites into her tote bag. Perhaps if a piece slid off her plate onto the napkin in her lap, and then the napkin happened to slide into the bag…

A side door near the front of the room opened, and a man Sadie didn't recognize hurried over to James Chalinder's chair. He leaned forward, cupped his hand, and appeared to speak for just a few seconds. Mr. Chalinder stood abruptly and followed the man out of the room. Other than a few swiveling heads at that first table, silverware continued to click against plates, and the meal proceeded as if nothing were awry. Sadie did her best to keep her curiosity in check, dividing her time between watching the crowd, nibbling on her food, and sneaking bits of game hen to Coco. Each bite was acknowledged with a tiny yip, which was easily muffled by the loud behavior of the three men at the table.

By the time dinner plates were removed and dessert served,

more than a few heads were glancing at the empty seat at the front table. A few guests leaned toward each other, exchanging comments.

"Something's not right," Sadie said, not bothering to whisper. Buddy, Marvin, and Jack weren't listening anyway as they were wrapped up in a snide criticism of a friend's golf abilities.

"What do you think is wrong?" Myrtle asked as she offered Sadie's tote bag a piece of her own game hen. "Is GQ not going to show up?"

"I think we're about to find out," Sadie said, nodding toward the front. James Chalinder had reentered the room. He appeared shaken yet calm as he approached the lectern.

"Ladies and gentlemen, I hope you are enjoying your dinner." He cleared his throat and repeated the collar-tugging motion Sadie had noticed earlier. "I'm afraid I have some bad news. Mr. Quinlan will not be able to join us this evening." Hushed comments circled the room, a mix of disappointment and questions. "There…" James Chalinder stopped again to clear his throat as his voice cracked. The hushed comments became a rumble of shock and questions. "I'm sorry, but I'm not able to give any more details." He turned and left quickly through the side door, followed by a woman and a couple of other men who'd been seated at the front table. All looked upset. Slowly guests at different tables stood and left as well, including the men at Sadie and Myrtle's table.

"This doesn't look good, does it?" Myrtle said, looking at Sadie, eyebrows raised.

"No," Sadie said. "This doesn't look good at all."

THREE

Sadie lingered in the dining hall, observing others who had attended the event. Some, disturbed by the announcement, left their desserts untouched and hurried from the room, almost as if whatever misfortune had befallen Garrison Quinlan might be contagious. Others remained, exchanging comments among themselves while tapping spoons on the fire-glazed surfaces of their crème brûlées.

"I think I'll retire," Myrtle said after a few bites of the sweet custard. "All this commotion is unsettling, and I hardly need a dessert on top of that fabulous meal." She patted one hip lightly.

"I understand completely," Sadie said, mimicking the gesture. "I'm already carrying around a few extra pounds of chocolate. It's my weakness."

Myrtle nodded. "Yes, mine too. I do love crème brûlée, but if they'd served a chocolate soufflé, I'd be scraping the bottom of the dish for every last morsel."

"Of course!" Sadie exclaimed. "Anything less would simply be unreasonable!" When it came to chocolate, there was never any hesitation. "Are you staying here at the hotel?"

"Yes," Myrtle said. "For the next three nights. You?"

"Several nights as well," Sadie replied. "We're on vacation." She glanced down at the tote bag, and Myrtle did the same, laughing in response. "Why don't we get together for coffee in the morning, say around nine?" Sadie suggested.

"Great idea," Myrtle agreed. "How about meeting at that espresso bar in the lobby?"

"Perfect," Sadie said.

The two women exchanged contact information in case plans changed. Sadie remained another ten minutes or so after her new friend departed, curious to see if the emcee emerged again or if anything else hinted at more information. Seeing no sign of additional activity, she picked up the Yorkie-laden tote bag and returned to her room.

* * *

"Such a strange turn of events, Coco, don't you think?" Sadie set the bag down on the hotel bed and lifted the petite canine out, gently placing her on the floor. Coco yipped twice in reply, an enthusiastic response. A single yip was more common.

Sadie sat down on the edge of the bed, kicked off her shoes, and wiggled her toes, pleased with the freedom. Eager to change into pajamas—her favorites, a pink flamingo print— she eyed Coco instead and fetched the Yorkie's rhinestone-studded leash. "I think a little venture outside would be a good idea before we settle in for the night." She clipped the leash to Coco's collar and escorted her to the room's sliding glass doors.

The access to the private garden patio and beach area was the best feature of the upscale accommodation in Sadie's opinion. Those who were inclined to gather together could easily use the main hallways, greeting others on their way to the hotel's bar, the Beach Bum, or common areas. Some vacationers loved to mingle, but Sadie viewed vacations as a chance to enjoy quiet time. She didn't need to travel in order to find crowds. San

Francisco offered plenty of opportunities to socialize.

Sliding open the glass doors, Sadie was surprised to find the ambiance not what she expected at all. The peace and quiet she and Coco had enjoyed earlier outside the room was now replaced with the chatter of other guests nearby. Multiple lights bounced along the ocean's edge, and a muffled but official-sounding voice on a megaphone mixed with the crashing waves.

"Oh dear," Sadie said, stepping forward onto the sand. She turned back and looped Coco's leash over the back of a lounge chair. "I think you'd better stay here," she said quietly, as if to calm Coco's nerves when it was really her own that were on edge.

Stepping beyond her room's private fenced area onto the beach, she found other guests had done the same. The chatter she'd heard when she first opened the sliding glass doors grew louder as she joined others from nearby rooms. Watching the activity at the water's edge, Sadie had a sinking feeling something was terribly wrong. Before she had a chance to approach any of the other guests on the beach, a man from the room next door called over to her.

"I heard they found a body," the man said.

Sadie walked closer to make sure she heard him correctly. "They found a *body?*"

"That's what everyone's saying," the man said. He nodded to the left and then the right, indicating others on the beach.

"When?" Sadie asked.

"I'd say about a half hour ago," the man replied. "At least that's when I heard shouting and came outside. My wife went to the front desk to see if she could find out what's going on." He looked back toward the room. "Here she comes now. Hopefully, she found something out."

A woman stepped out of the couple's hotel room and joined her husband on the sand. "The front desk can't tell me anything. But a coroner's vehicle just pulled up outside."

Not a good sign, Sadie said to herself.

"A coroner's vehicle?" the man asked as if he wasn't sure he'd heard correctly.

"And a media van," the woman added.

Really, really not a good sign…

"Accidental drowning perhaps?" Sadie said, trying to take a positive route. As if an accidental drowning could be considered positive. But it beat a whole slew of other alternatives.

"Could be," the woman said. "Swimming after dark would be dangerous, especially without a lifeguard around. I'm Julie, by the way, and this is my husband, Tom."

Sadie followed with her own introduction. She excused herself for a moment to retrieve Coco from the patio. Unhooking the leash from the lounge chair, she returned to the conversation, Coco contentedly tucked into her arms. Several police officers arrived, joining others already there. They spread themselves across the beach to keep people away from the scene.

"This is crazy," Julie said. "You see those two arguing over there?" An officer was involved in a heated exchange with a cameraman who was attempting to access the beach with film equipment.

"Each just trying to do his job," Tom pointed out. "The police should come first, though, in view of the situation."

"You're right," Julie said. "But the media? That makes me wonder… Oh my! You know that celebrity is staying here, right?"

"What celebrity?" Tom said, only half-attentive.

"The *GQ* guy, Tom," Julie said, her voice getting animated. "I wonder if that's why media people are showing up? Do you think…? Oh, it couldn't be!"

"This would bring the media out in any case, celebrity or not," Sadie pointed out quickly. It was true, and she wasn't about to cough up the information that "the *GQ* guy" hadn't shown up to the dinner. There would be enough rumors floating around without adding fuel. Julie's voice had already doubled in volume. It wouldn't be long before others began coming over to get the latest information. *Even if it happens to be true…*

Using Coco as a reason to excuse herself—"I must take this little darling inside before she gets cold!"—Sadie retired to her room. There was no point in lingering around what promised to be an escalating situation.

Leaving the sliding glass door cracked enough to be able to hear any developments, Sadie pulled the curtain closed for privacy and changed into her favorite pajamas. She washed her face and applied a layer of Wink-a-Wrink to her skin. Twisting her head from side to side, she debated the reflection in the mirror. The ostensibly miraculous cream had been a late-night infomercial discovery—*Wrinkles vanish in a wink with Wink-a-Wrink!* So far, no amount of winking had made any visible difference. She brought one hand to her face, ran her fingers along the side of her cheek, and shrugged. Figuring there was nothing to lose, she applied an extra layer.

"What do you think, Coco?" Sadie sat down on the edge of the bed and patted the tops of her flamingo-covered thighs. The Yorkie quickly hopped up from the floor where she'd been watching the nightly ritual. She propped herself up on Sadie's lap and cocked her furry head to one side. "No, not about the wrinkles," Sadie said. "But about all this hullaballoo on the beach." Seemingly without an opinion, Coco curled up in Sadie's lap and closed her eyes.

Not one to argue with a good suggestion, Sadie moved Coco to her comfortable travel palace, fluffing the velvet pillow. Returning to bed, she slipped between the hotel's luxurious eight-hundred-thread-count sheets. In spite of the distant hum of activity in the distance, she fell asleep.

FOUR

Myrtle was already seated in the coffee area of the lobby when Sadie arrived the following morning. Having tossed and turned with odd dreams during the night, Sadie was barely awake.

Myrtle, however, was bright-eyed and clearly caffeinated. She waved one hand enthusiastically as she watched Sadie approach. "Did you hear?" she whispered after Sadie ordered a café au lait at the espresso bar and then took a seat.

Sadie nodded. "I heard *and* saw," she said.

"You saw the body?" Myrtle gasped.

"No. I saw the activity on the beach," Sadie said. Hearing her name called out, she stood and walked back to the counter to pick up her drink.

"You must have one of the ocean-view suites," Myrtle said, having considered Sadie's statement by the time she returned to the table.

Sadie took an initial sip of café au lait and set the cup down. "Yes, I do. And there was quite a commotion outside the suite when we returned from dinner." She glanced at her tote bag, as did Myrtle. Sadie imagined Coco would be content to have her presence acknowledged. At this thought, she went back to the counter and picked up a cranberry orange scone, dropping a nibble into the tote when she finally sat down again. "Isn't that right, Coco?" A muddled yip followed—a scone-altered reply.

"There were voices outside when we stepped onto the patio," Sadie explained. "Other guests were on the beach, discussing the scene."

"Which was what?" Myrtle prodded. "I have a garden-view room, so I can't see the beach. You must have seen everything!"

"Not really," Sadie said. "It was all down by the shoreline. But I could see flashlights, and there were police keeping people back from the scene. One reporter in particular was giving an officer a bad time while trying to get closer."

"Well, reporters need to get the story one way or another," Myrtle said. "Perhaps getting close is what they have to do even if they don't get much to report." She pushed a newspaper across the table to Sadie. "Local paper. Check out the front page."

Sadie took a look at the headline: "Body Found on the Beach." A short article followed. "They must have barely had time to slip this in before it hit the press."

"I imagine so," Myrtle said, taking another gulp of her coffee.

"Do they say who it was?" Sadie asked.

Myrtle shook her head. "No. It says the identity is not yet confirmed and that it won't be released to the public until notification of next of kin."

"That's normal procedure," Sadie pointed out.

"Yes," Myrtle agreed. "But it also mentions that Garrison Quinlan did not show up for a dinner engagement here last night. Which you and I already know."

Sadie sipped her drink and contemplated that. Naturally, the paper would drop hints to make the article catchy. It was what the media did. But she already suspected the deceased was the missing-in-action celebrity. Why else would he have not shown up when he was the guest of honor? It seemed the most likely explanation, unfortunately for all his adoring fans. And, needless to say, for him.

"I'm very curious about this," Myrtle said. She placed her elbows on the table and rested her chin on clasped hands. "I just can't resist a good mystery."

Sadie's eyebrows shot up. She'd recognized a kindred spirit in the woman from the start, but this confirmed it. "Exactly! I know the feeling well."

"Really?" Myrtle regarded Sadie with a new look of appreciation.

"Oh yes!" Sadie exclaimed. "It has landed me in trouble more than once."

"Tell me about it!" Myrtle said, shaking her head. "I've even been a person of interest at times."

Sadie laughed, thinking about several similar situations she'd found herself in before.

Sadie and Myrtle stopped talking as two younger women slid into seats at a table nearby. The newcomers appeared to be in their early twenties. Glittered manicures wrapped around sizable drinks that Sadie suspected were some sort of tall-half-caf-nonfat-soy-no-foam-latte something or others.

"I just can't believe it!" one of the women said. A blue streak of hair fell forward as she leaned toward her companion. "It's all over Twitter!"

"I *refuse* to believe it." The other woman shook her head, wild black curls flying side to side as her nose ring reflected the ceiling lights. Sadie could hear the threat of tears in the woman's voice. "I love him! He can't be gone!"

"I love him too!" A glittery finger wiped away a tear. "And to think we traveled all this way just to see him!"

Sadie glanced at Myrtle, eyebrows raised. *Not to mention the little detail that he might be dead...*

———

"Well, you can't trust everything you read on Twitter." The blue-haired woman blew across the opening of her to-go cup and then took a cautious sip.

"You're right," her companion said. "Let's check Facebook." She set her drink down, picked her cell phone up off the table, touched the surface, and started scrolling.

Sadie fought back the urge to laugh.

As the conversation at the next table continued, Myrtle tapped Sadie's hand and gestured toward the counter. Two of the men who'd been seated at their dinner table the night before had joined the line. "Look," she whispered. "Rude guys if you ask me."

"No argument there," Sadie agreed. "I wonder where the third one is."

"He may have checked out already," Myrtle suggested.

"Possibly," Sadie said. "Or he might not even have been a guest here. Not everyone who attends an event stays overnight at the location."

Myrtle nodded. "True."

"On the other hand…" Sadie tilted her head, indicating a chair across the lobby. The third man from the trio was standing near a chair occupied by none other than James Chalinder. "Look over there."

As both Sadie and Myrtle watched, the rude dinner companion—*companion* being quite the exaggeration— pointed to a folded newspaper in the manager's lap. Obviously done reading it, Chalinder offered it to the man, who tucked it under his arm and joined the other two men in the coffee line.

"Seems everyone's interested in the headlines this morning," Myrtle said.

"Can't blame them for that," Sadie said. "It was the first

thing I looked for myself."

Raised voices floated across from another section of the lobby, and Sadie and Myrtle turned their attention toward the commotion. A suit-clad man with a name tag on was attempting to move a man holding a camera away from the front desk. The clerk behind the counter was motioning for the next person in line to step forward.

"Hotel management has its work cut out today, I bet," Myrtle said.

Sadie nodded. Between the media and the celebrity's fans, it was guaranteed to be a chaotic day.

A buzz from Sadie's cell phone indicated an incoming text. Glancing at the screen, she smiled. *Detective Broussard.* The New Orleans detective had become both a good friend and… dare she admit it… a romantic interest.

Ms. Kramer.

Detective Broussard.

Sadie enjoyed the formal salutations they used before launching into more familiar language.

I thought I'd check in to see how your trip is going. Broussard's text sounded casual, but Sadie could read between the lines. He'd undoubtedly heard the news and heard the location. And she *had* told him where she'd be staying. Of course he'd connect the dots.

Fine, Sadie texted back. *A lovely hotel. A few interesting details.*

Like a dead celebrity? That kind of detail?

Just as she suspected. *Seems to be the prevailing theory,* she responded.

A theory is just a theory until there's a positive ID.

Sadie held the phone up so Myrtle could see the conversation. "A detective friend," she whispered, realizing immediately how silly it was to lower her voice. A person texting obviously could not hear through the phone.

Myrtle leaned forward and read the texts. She nodded enthusiastically as if being let in on inside information. After reading, she leaned back in her chair and took a sip of coffee.

Turning the phone back toward herself, Sadie added a quick response. *Of course, theory is just theory. But facts are there somewhere.*

Yes, for the police to find.

Again, Sadie could read between the lines. This was Broussard's polite way of telling her to stay out of it. Not that she intended to heed his subtle words of caution.

Naturally. Sadie sent off the one-word text and glanced up at the ever-changing sounds of activity in the hotel lobby. This time she watched as two official-looking men approached the front desk.

"Look," Sadie said to Myrtle, nodding toward the officers. She followed with a quick text to Broussard. *I think some detectives just arrived.*

May I ask a favor?

Sadie could picture the smirk on Broussard's face even several states away.

Never hurts to ask, Sadie replied.

Let them do their job.

Sadie tapped one finger against her cheek, searching for a perfectly noncommittal response. *As a favor to them?*

Yes. And as a favor to me.

Sadie looked up from her phone and noticed the officers had started talking with a few people in the lobby. *They may want to question me*, Sadie typed.

Why?

Sadie sighed. *Because I was there at the dinner.*

Really? I thought you were just going for vacation, not for a celebrity event.

So did I. But there was an invitation in my check-in packet. She smiled and then added, *I wasn't about to turn away a free dinner.*

Understandable. I would have done the same.

Sadie clucked her tongue in satisfaction, a gesture that caused Myrtle to raise her eyebrows. They exchanged smirks, at the same time noticing the detectives were headed in their direction, toward the coffee area in general. Noting that the younger women at the next table had already left, she and Myrtle were the likely targets.

Gotta go, Sadie typed, anticipating an interruption. *Will touch base later.*

FIVE

Sadie ended the text exchange with Broussard and slipped her phone into her tote bag. She paused to pat Coco on the head before removing her hand. Sure enough, after speaking with the barista, presumably to explain their presence, the two men approached Sadie and Myrtle.

"Good morning, ladies. Do you mind if we ask you a couple of questions?"

The fortyish man who spoke was accompanied by a man at least a decade his junior.

"Have a seat," Myrtle offered, indicating two empty chairs at the table.

"Thank you, but that won't be necessary," the older man said. "This won't take long. I'm Detective Martin, and this is Detective Sloan. We're speaking with any guests who happened to attend the dinner event here last night. Any chance you two were there?"

"As a matter of fact, we were," Sadie said. Whimsically, Sadie thought the combination of names might make a good business: Martin and Sloan. Perhaps they should consider starting a private PI agency.

"Good," the same officer said, clearly pleased with the answer. He pulled a pad of paper and pen from his pocket and prepared to take notes. "Were you sitting close to the front?"

Sadie shook her head. "No. In fact, we were at the very back, the last table."

The detective looked visibly disappointed. "I see," he said. "Did you happen to observe anything that might be of importance? Was anyone acting oddly?"

"Yes," Myrtle said abruptly. "Three very rude men sat at the table with us. Didn't even introduce themselves. Hotshots, I guess."

"More like wannabe hotshots," Sadie clarified, glancing at Myrtle. "Those are the ones who usually put on airs." A yip from the tote followed as if Coco agreed with Sadie's opinion.

"Hollywood types," the younger detective muttered.

"Anything else?" Detective Martin asked. He cast a quick glance at Sadie's bag.

"Actually, yes," Sadie said. "Even though we were at the back of the room, I could see the front table clearly, the one I assume was reserved for the guest of honor. The man who emceed the event sat at that table with an empty seat beside him."

"You say he emceed the event." Detective Martin jotted down a note. "How did he seem when making announcements?"

"Perfectly fine early on," Sadie said.

"Until that man came in and whispered something to him," Myrtle added.

Detective Martin frowned. "You could tell he whispered from that far away?"

Sadie sat up a little straighter. "Well, he might have leaned forward, cupped his hand around the man's ear, and then shouted."

"There's no need for sarcasm, ma'am," Detective Martin said.

"My late husband and I had a dog that would do that," Sadie said, turning her attention to Myrtle. "She'd sneak up to the bed in the morning, put her nose in one of our ears, and bark."

"Quite the alarm clock!" Myrtle exclaimed.

"Indeed." Sadie nodded.

Both women turned back to face Detective Martin when he cleared his throat.

"My impression," Sadie said, assuming a more serious tone, "was that whatever the man said upset the emcee terribly. He was barely able to announce that the celebrity would not be able to make it."

"And then what happened?"

"He rushed from the room," Sadie said.

"Do you have any idea who the man was that came into the room and *whispered* to him?"

Sadie was delighted to hear a touch of sarcasm in Detective Martin's question. Her estimation of him went up several notches. Unfortunately, she didn't have an answer. "No."

"A description?"

Sadie shook her head. "No, I wasn't really paying attention until I saw the way the emcee reacted. By then, the other man had exited the side door."

"Clothing?"

"Yes, of course!" Sadie said. She and Myrtle exchanged faux-shocked glances.

"What *kind* of clothing was he wearing?" Detective Martin tapped his pen against the notepad.

"Some sort of suit, like every other man there," Sadie said.

"Do you remember if he was wearing an outdoor jacket?" This came from the younger detective. Detective Martin gave him a look that Sadie took to be approval. Sadie approved too. It was a good question.

"I don't think so," Sadie said. "But it's summer. I don't see why he'd have a jacket over his suit even if he came in from outside."

"It's too warm for jackets," Myrtle said.

Detective Martin nodded. "I agree." He directed the next question at Sadie. "Why did you say 'even if he came in from outside'?"

Sadie leaned forward, adopting a more serious tone. "To use an old cliché, isn't there an elephant in the room that we're stepping around? Let's get to the point behind your questions. We all know a body washed up on the beach last night, and it's most likely that of Garrison Quinlan. I'm in an oceanfront suite. Many of us ended up outside, standing on the sand, watching the commotion. It was quite a scene."

"I'm well aware of that," Detective Martin said. "I was there." He scribbled another note and then looked up. "Do you recall anyone watching who didn't seem to be one of the hotel guests? Someone alone, not interacting with others?"

Sadie thought back to the night before, visualizing the crowds along the stretch of oceanfront rooms. The guests she'd met and talked to were certainly not standing back. And others nearby seemed to be gathered in clusters. "I don't think so," she said. "People were just trying to find out from each other what was going on."

"Are you saying this was a crime?" Myrtle piped up, her tone animated. She turned to Sadie. "You know criminals sometimes return to the scene of the crime. Why, just the other day on CSI—"

Detective Martin cleared his throat again.

"We're simply investigating at this point," the younger detective said.

"Exactly," Martin said. He clicked his pen and slid both the pen and the notebook into his pocket. "That'll be all for now, ladies. Thank you for your cooperation." The two detectives turned and walked away, scanning the lobby for any other potential sources of information.

"What do you think?" Myrtle turned to Sadie, eyebrows raised.

"I'm thinking foul play," Sadie said. "Why else would they be questioning people? Then again, it could have been an accident."

Myrtle took a sip of coffee and drummed her fingers on the table. "You think he just decided to go swimming? Got caught in a riptide and drowned?"

"It's possible, I suppose," Sadie said. "Still, it seems odd to me that he'd go swimming right before he had an engagement."

"We don't know how long the body had been in the water," Myrtle pointed out.

"Good point," Sadie said. "He might have gone out much earlier."

"How could we find that out?"

"How, indeed," Sadie said, echoing Myrtle's question. "It's too soon for those details to be in the morning paper."

"But maybe not online," Myrtle suggested. "Those girls with the glittery fingernails said they'd read about it online. I wish I were more internet-savvy. I'd try to find out."

Sadie nodded. "I'm a little old-school when it comes to social media too. But I know someone who is up to speed: my assistant. I'll call her now."

SIX

The phone rang four times before Amber picked up.

"Busy morning?" Sadie asked, knowing her assistant was usually quick on the draw when it came to answering the boutique phone.

"Not really," Amber said. "We've had some customers browsing but no sales. I was just retrieving go-backs from the dressing room."

"Aha," Sadie said. "Well, at least they're looking."

"True," Amber said. "And sometimes they'll come back for things they've tried on. One woman really loved that fuzzy purple chenille sweater on the sale rack." A clicking of hangers followed. Sadie knew by the sound that Amber was carrying the cordless phone around the shop while returning items to racks. "What's up? Are things crazy at the hotel? Lots of activity? Any more news?"

"Not really," Sadie said. "Some detectives came by and asked questions but didn't offer any information. We were hoping you could fill us in."

"We?" Amber asked.

"Myrtle, a new friend," Sadie explained. "Anything new you've read on the internet?"

"Not really," Amber said. "Just posts from people saying they love him, and some photos of candles, cards, and posters outside his Bel Air estate. But I was thinking…"

"What?" Sadie glanced at Myrtle, whose eyes widened at

the possibility of new information.

"I don't like to speculate," Amber said, her voice hesitant. "But he's been having all those personal problems lately. It could be… Oh, I hate to suggest it."

Sadie picked up on Amber's thoughts quickly, wondering why she hadn't considered the possibility herself. "You think he took his own life?"

Amber choked up. "I don't know."

"What personal problems?" Sadie had overlooked the fact that Amber kept up on the tabloids. Not that half of what was printed there was true, but a few tidbits probably were. And personal problems could lead to all kinds of situations. *Like murder, for example…*

"Some sort of stalker situation," Amber said. "He'd taken out a restraining order."

"A stalker situation," Sadie repeated aloud so Myrtle could hear. "Well, that certainly isn't good."

"No," Amber said. "And there's that paternity suit."

"Paternity suit," Sadie echoed. "Also not good."

"Plus the bankruptcy rumors," Amber continued.

"Bankruptcy rumors…" Sadie was beginning to feel like a gossip even though she was only repeating the information Amber was giving her so that Myrtle could hear.

"But everyone *loved* him!" Amber gushed.

Sadie leaned back in her chair and fiddled with her coffee cup. "Not everyone, Amber. You don't have those kinds of problems without an enemy here or there." *Most likely here,* Sadie thought, glancing around the hotel lobby. "Anything else?" Not that Amber's revelations weren't enough already.

"Well, there was also the paparazzi incident a few weeks ago."

"What paparazzi incident?"

Amber sighed. "You didn't see that on *Today's Entertainment Trivia?*"

"I pretty much stick to *Columbo* reruns," Sadie said. "What happened?"

"Those people follow him everywhere. He pushed a guy out of the way when the guy blocked him from getting into his Ferrari," Amber said. "So the paparazzi dude sued him for assault. And he countersued for harassment. You should see that car. Bright red. Such a gorgeous ride!"

"He might have gone with something lower key if he wanted to go unnoticed," Sadie suggested. "Less flashy."

"Maybe he needed to keep his image up," Amber suggested. "That last issue of *Hot Stars* magazine had a cover photo of him leaning against that car."

"*Hot Stars* magazine, you say?" Sadie held back a chuckle. "I guess I missed that."

Myrtle shook her head, smiling. "A gossip rag," she whispered.

"Well, it does sound like the man had a boatload of problems, Amber," Sadie said. "I can see why you think he might have taken his own life. But I'm leaning more toward the enemy theory. If it *was* murder, that is. It also could have been accidental."

The sound of a chime told Sadie that a customer had entered the boutique. Thanking Amber for the tabloid tidbits, she ended the call, then looked at Myrtle and shrugged her shoulders.

"Any leads there?" Myrtle said. "It sounds like your assistant keeps track of the entertainment headlines. Must be some kind of clues mixed in with the usual hype and gibberish."

"Probably," Sadie said. "But I can't see how, not without more information. Mr. Quinlan certainly had some stress in his life, if the stories are true."

Myrtle nodded. "I'm sure he did. Celebrity life isn't all glamour like some people think." She downed the rest of her coffee and set the empty cup on the table. "You did say something that got me thinking though."

"What's that?" Sadie also finished off her drink and set the cup next to Myrtle's.

"The boatload," Myrtle said.

Sadie frowned, thinking. "What boatload?"

"The boatload of problems," Myrtle said. "It just made me wonder how he ended up in the water. Did he just go for a swim? Or was he on some boat or watercraft and had an accident?"

"Or a nonaccident," Sadie pointed out.

"Yes." Myrtle drummed her fingers on the table with one hand. Her chin rested on the other hand, elbow propped up on the table. "But why would he have been out on a boat when he had an event? And what boat? I haven't seen any boat rentals around here."

"They do have some day excursions north of here," Sadie said. "I once took one out of Long Beach. We were back in time to make it to a dinner engagement."

"That's a possibility then," Myrtle said.

"Well, there aren't any details yet," Sadie said. "Hopefully, there'll be more on the news tonight. We might have some indication of what he was doing yesterday afternoon, or at least if they suspect foul play."

"We could try grilling the detectives for more information." Myrtle tilted her head toward a corner of the lobby where Martin and Sloan were speaking with a middle-aged couple.

Sadie smiled. "I must say, irritating the officers investigating a crime seems to be one of my fortes. I'm rather experienced at it. And I dare say I enjoy it at times.”

“Understandable!” Myrtle agreed. “We all need a little mischief in our lives, don’t we?”

“Absolutely,” Sadie said. “But… these two don’t seem to have much of a sense of humor. I doubt we’ll get any information from them. I say we wait for the news tonight.”

Myrtle tilted her head to the side, eyeing the officers. “You’re right. Perhaps I’ll try lingering within earshot. I could peruse books on that rounder at the front of the gift shop or pretend to be searching for lost sunglasses near their conversations. It won’t seem obvious, and I might overhear something.”

“Now you’re thinking,” Sadie said. “Speaking of hearing, I seem to hear the boardwalk shops calling my name.” She glanced in her tote bag. “Isn’t that right, Coco?” An affirmative yip followed.

“I’ll catch up to you later,” Myrtle said. She stood and pushed her chair back under the table.

Sadie also stood. “There’s a cocktail hour with appetizers from five to six later on.”

“Wouldn’t miss it! See you there.” Myrtle took off for the gift shop, waving one hand over her shoulder as she walked away.

Sadie looped the handle of her tote over her shoulder and swung the bag slightly to the front to keep Coco close. “Let’s hit the boardwalk, Coco.” Smiling at the yip that followed, she headed for the hotel’s front door. After all, what was a beach vacation without a little shopping?

SEVEN

The boardwalk area bustled with activity, half the crowd heading toward the sand, the other half simply walking or browsing beachside businesses. A few people rested on benches, nibbling on funnel cake. A couple dressed in athletic wear jogged past at a medium pace. The atmosphere was light and carefree with the easygoing ambiance created by people with free time on their hands.

Sales racks outside shops stood ready to lure people inside with colorful cover-ups and swimsuits. Always a fan of accessorizing, one small storefront caught Sadie's eye immediately. Never one to pass up an opportunity to shop, Sadie headed for the small front doorway and stepped inside.

Bertie's Beach Baubles was aptly named. Wall hooks displayed dangling strands of seashells, bright beads, and whimsical figures of every shape and variety: mermaids, pink flamingos, jungle animals in bathing suits, neon beach balls, metallic surfboards, and more.

"Look, Coco," Sadie said, fingering one particular strand. "Dogs with sunglasses on!" Coco popped up and peeked over the edge of the tote bag. Seemingly unimpressed, she retreated back inside.

"Don't worry, I understand," Sadie said. "What would you do with a clunky necklace six times your height? Not exactly practical, is it?" She moved along from one design to the next, fingering the textures and shapes of tiki-type cocktail drinks, miniature snorkeling gear, beach hats, palm trees, and the requisite seashell, starfish, and seahorse designs.

"So many choices!" a woman's voice chirped.

Sadie looked up at the sound of the unexpected comment, realizing she'd been so fascinated with the necklaces that she'd almost run right into another customer. Dressed in shorts, a tank top, baseball cap, and sunglasses, the young woman looked like half the people on the boardwalk, yet something about her struck Sadie as familiar. "Yes, indeed!" Sadie quipped. "I simply can't choose! Then again…" She lifted up a necklace with a repetitive pattern of brightly colored miniature flip-flops. Holding it in front of her chest, she looked in the shop mirror and nodded with approval. "This will do just fine."

"You have excellent taste," the woman said, her tone cheerful, almost sugary. She pulled a matching flip-flop necklace off the rack and added one each of the cocktail drinks and beach hats. "Perfect," she said. "Well, I think I'll take that one too. It's darling." She added a necklace with diminutive suitcases. "Wonderful for a getaway trip!" she said. With a brief goodbye smile, she took her purchases to the sales counter and paid.

"Vacationers are so cheerful," Sadie said to no one in particular after the woman left the store. "In fact, I feel it too; it's contagious!" Wandering to a shelf display not far from the sales counter, Sadie picked a bracelet from a basket of varied patterns and held it up. "Look, Coco, these match the necklaces on the wall racks. And there's one with dogs wearing sunglasses! This would work for you!" Coco's head emerged slowly from the tote bag and tilted her head, giving the item a cautious inspection.

"And it's thin elastic," the clerk, a young woman Sadie

guessed to be an older teen, pointed out. "So if it catches on anything, it will break."

Sadie eyed the salesgirl, eyebrows raised. "Ah, I see. Not a great selling point for humans, but…"

The girl smiled and nodded. "Yes, a good safety feature for dogs."

"Coco does like to be fashionable," Sadie said. "Isn't that right, Coco?" The Yorkie sniffed the bracelet in seeming approval. "We'll take it. And let's add another one with flip-flops. That way we can match." She placed both bracelets and the necklace on the sales counter and took a brief stroll around the rest of the shop in case there was anything else she might want to add. The variety was mind-boggling—everything from purple octopus earrings to toe rings bearing giant fuchsia starfish. Sand candles, scarves, refrigerator magnets, and dozens of other whimsical items rounded out the shop offerings. Sadie picked out a beach-themed suncatcher and returned to the sales counter.

"Those suncatchers are cool," the salesgirl said as she rang up the total. "You can hang them in your window or use them for Christmas ornaments." Sadie noticed her name tag read Bertie and wondered if she had misjudged the young woman's age.

"You must be Bertie," Sadie said, nodding toward the name tag.

"No." The girl laughed. "That's my mom's name tag. I just help out during college breaks."

"Ah, that makes sense," Sadie said, withholding the urge to sigh. It was just as she thought; the older she got, the younger everyone else looked.

Paying for her purchases, she placed them in her tote carefully, making sure not to drop anything on Coco's head.

She'd made that mistake before and suffered an extensive yipped lecture.

The boardwalk grew more crowded as Sadie continued on. Cheers and shouts drifted over from a volleyball game, and grunts and groans accompanied determined athletes at a workout area on the sand. Vendor carts offered hot dogs, fresh fruit, and giant pretzels. Sadie made a note to come back to an especially enticing kiosk with the name Surf 'N Sorbet printed on a horizontal surfboard above the counter. A vertical boogie board off to the side announced the flavor choices of the day.

Slender young women in skimpy bikinis hovered flirtatiously near the muscle-builders. An older trio of women held and discussed books at an outdoor café patio, wide-brimmed hats protecting their faces from sun damage. Everywhere she looked, the beachside scene buzzed with activity.

"My," Sadie said aloud as she paused in front of a surfboard shop. She ran her hand across an impressive design of pink hyacinths on a shimmering blue background. The smooth varnished surface was cool against her skin, a welcome contrast to the growing heat of the day. "Now, I wouldn't mind a dress made out of that. Don't you think so, Coco?" She addressed the question directly to her tote bag. "It would match perfectly with those turquoise earrings I picked up in Taos a few years ago."

A cough alerted her to the fact someone had overheard her musings. She looked up to see a young man leaning in the doorway. His blond hair, T-shirt with the words Surf's Up on the front, and pendant with what looked like a shark's tooth, took her right back to her Beach Boys days. Ah, how she'd loved that music. She'd often thought of "Fun, Fun, Fun" as her personal theme song. "Little Deuce Coupe" reminded her of her own red Mustang convertible. And when, two decades later, "Kokomo" emerged on the music scene, she was thrilled.

"I'm not sure fiberglass would be comfortable to wear." The sly grin that accompanied the remark let Sadie know it was playful teasing. "At least not with epoxy on it," he added.

"You have a good point there, young man," Sadie said. "I'll just have to stick to the beachwear shops for my clothing purchases."

"Looks like you brought a young surfer with you though."

Confused, Sadie looked over her shoulder before realizing Coco had stuck her head out of the tote at the sound of a stranger's voice. The Yorkie chose to show her appreciation for the surfing suggestion by licking the board in question. Twice.

"Sorry about that," Sadie said, apologizing for Coco's lack of manners. "Maybe she has a secret desire to surf."

"Doesn't everyone?"

Sadie laughed, deciding to take the question as rhetorical, though perhaps it was serious. "I'm guessing you surf."

The young man nodded. "Every second that I'm not working or sleeping. I usually get a couple of hours in before work. Well, not this morning."

"Not this morning?" Sadie raised an eyebrow.

"No." The surfer looked out at the ocean, frowning. "They say a body washed up on the beach last night. Creepy! I usually surf before work, but like I said, creepy."

"Yes, that's understandable." *Creepy indeed.* "I heard that news too. I don't think I'd want to go out in the water, at least not right away," Sadie said. Not one to miss a chance to take advantage of local knowledge, Sadie pushed for any additional information the young surfer might be able to provide. "Do you have any idea what happened?"

The young man shrugged his shoulders. "Only what everyone's saying. That it was that *GQ* hotshot that all the girls go wild over. Drowned or something."

"Yes," Sadie said. *Or something.* "I guess a lot of people go swimming here." She looked over at the beach, observing crowds by the water.

"Yeah, but if he drowned without anyone seeing, it probably wasn't right here."

"Really?" Sadie raised both eyebrows.

"The currents run north to south."

"I see," Sadie said, thinking it over. "So if time passed after he drowned…"

"He would have floated here from somewhere else. Like I said, creepy." He looked up as an attractive girl zoomed by on a skateboard. "Go, Stacey!" he called out. "Crazy chick from my high school," he added as if owing Sadie an explanation.

Seeing the "crazy chick from high school" circling back to talk to the young surfer, Sadie excused herself and walked back to Surf 'N Sorbet. One purchase of Mango Madness in a waffle cup later, she sat down on a bench to enjoy the frozen concoction and shot a text off to her favorite detective.

Detective Broussard.

Ms. Kramer.

As always, Sadie smiled at their formal greetings. She set Coco on the ground and looped the Yorkie's pink rhinestone leash around her wrist, giving the petite canine freedom to sniff around and herself freedom to type.

The ocean current here runs north to south, she texted.

Yes, that's correct.

Sadie sighed. Was she the only one who didn't know this? She always knew she should have paid more attention in science classes.

So a body that washed up here would have started traveling north of here.

There was a delay before a return text came through. Sadie took a taste of the sorbet balanced behind her cell phone and braced for a lecture on staying uninvolved, and she was relieved to get a simple response.

If it traveled, that's a reasonable assumption. The current along the California coast would not carry it northbound.

Pleased with this information, Sadie still wasn't sure how it would tie in with GQ's situation. But it stood to reason that anything washing up on a beach would be affected by the ocean currents.

What happened to enjoying your beach vacation?

Sadie could envision Broussard grinning. *I happen to be sitting by the ocean enjoying sorbet as we speak, er, text.* As if to emphasize her statement, she finished off the Mango Madness. She tossed the remaining half of the cone in a nearby trash container, figuring she'd save a few calories that way.

You're way ahead of me there. I'm sitting at a police station desk writing reports. I'd be happy to trade places.

Sadie smiled as she typed. *I'll have to think about that. I suspect my view is better.*

A safe bet, Broussard sent back.

I'll let you go then. Maybe I'll see if the hotel spa has openings. The idea only struck her as she typed, but it certainly seemed like a good one.

Again, happy to trade places with you.

Sadie finished texting, helped Coco back into her tote, and took off for the hotel.

EIGHT

Sadie fluffed the pillows on her hotel bed and lay back against them. Relaxed from grabbing a last-minute cancellation at the spa, it took some effort just to lift the remote control to the television. But, determined to hear the five-o'clock news, she clicked it on. Certainly by now the police would have more information about the previous night's events. Sure enough, it was the lead story. The attractive female news anchor set aside a paper and faced the camera with a professional yet grim expression.

Our top story tonight brings updated news concerning the body that washed up on the shore last night. Police have released the name of the deceased as well-known celebrity Garrison Quinlan following identification by his personal manager, James Chalinder. Mr. Quinlan was to have made a guest of honor appearance at a dinner at the hotel Casa Playa but did not show up for the event. It is not known at this time if foul play is suspected. Police are not releasing any additional details pending an investigation. We will keep you updated as new information becomes available.

"Well, Coco, what do you think of that?" Sadie reached for a bottle of water she'd pulled from the room's refrigerator when she returned from the spa. She took a sip and set it back down on the night table beside the bed. "That must have been a terrible ordeal for Mr. Chalinder. He was obviously distressed when he ran from the ballroom last night. Don't you think so, Coco?" Sadie shuddered at the thought of having to identify any body, much less one belonging to a close work associate. Coco, on the other hand, seemed more concerned with her favorite toy, a stuffed red lobster that had accompanied them on the trip.

The room phone rang, and Sadie picked it up on the second ring, already knowing who would be on the other end of the call.

"Did you see the news?" Myrtle said.

"Yes, terrible," Sadie said. "But not much more than we already figured."

"Still terrible." Myrtle coughed, and Sadie realized she heard the chattering of voices in the background.

"Where are you?" Sadie glanced at her watch, noting it was almost six o'clock.

"The reception in the lobby," Myrtle said. "I'm on the house phone. Are you coming down?"

Sadie sat up and swung her legs over the side of the bed. "I can't believe I forgot. I just got back from the spa about a half hour ago. Seems it drained my memory as well as my stress."

"Oh, I'm jealous," Myrtle said. "I would have chosen that over this reception hour. Nothing but clusters of wealthy people gossiping and scarfing up the food. Speaking of which, they're running low, but I can still grab some appetizers for you. The mini-taquitos are delicious."

"Well, I can't resist mini-taquitos," Sadie exclaimed. "I'll throw something on and be right down. Is there an avocado sauce to go with them?" She started for the closet but stopped when an abrupt tug reminded her she wasn't on a cordless phone.

"The best ever," Myrtle confirmed. "Sort of a mix

between guacamole and salsa." A crunching sound followed, presumably to let Sadie know what she was missing.

"Be right there." Sadie hung up the phone and rummaged through the clothing choices in her closet. If only she hadn't spent so much time at Bertie's Beach Baubles and talking with the young surfer, she might have had time to pick up something new at a beachside boutique. However, she never traveled without options. She tossed on a bright yellow tunic and black slacks. Fluffing her hair with a brush, she added the new flip-flop necklace and a favorite pair of black-and-yellow-striped clip-on earrings. Adorning Coco with her own new necklace of dogs with sunglasses, the two headed for the lobby.

Myrtle was easy to spot, even as crowded as the cocktail hour gathering was. She clearly had Sadie's funky fashion taste—quite unique and clever, if Sadie had her say about it—and was decked out in a ruffled white blouse with hot-pink polka dots and a flowing skirt in a similar pink shade. Her earlobes sparkled with flashy earrings too far away to specifically identify.

Sadie worked her way through the crowd with numerous utterances of "Excuse me" until she finally stood beside Myrtle. So taken by the flashing lighthouse-design earrings, she almost forgot to say hello. She made a mental note to find out who the manufacturer was so she could order them in for Flair.

"There you are!" Myrtle said. She handed Sadie an appetizer plate with mini-taquitos and avocado sauce. "I grabbed these for you since they were disappearing quickly. I don't know if they'll put more out or not."

"Excellent thinking, thanks," Sadie said. "Anything interesting going on here?"

"Just people-watching," Myrtle said. "And listening to the chatter. Lots of comments about GQ."

———

Sadie nodded while biting into a mini-taquito. "I can imagine," she said once she had a chance to swallow. "Some of these people must have been here for the dinner event last night."

"Unless they just checked in. Those oafs were certainly here." Myrtle pointed toward the open bar. The rude men from their table stood laughing as they flaunted their rocks glasses, swirling the contents in a circular manner.

"And I see Martin and Sloan are here," Sadie said, nodding toward the detectives they'd spoken with in the coffee area that morning.

Myrtle nodded. "I saw that. Seems they're observing more than talking to people this time."

"Looking for any behavior that seems out of the ordinary, I bet." Sadie glanced around the room, noting that it appeared to be an appetizer hour like any other. She'd been to many while traveling. After all, why miss free food? Not to mention the intrigue of people-watching.

Sadie took another bite and then made a quick trip to the serving table, as much to mingle and overhear conversations as to nab another mini-taquito. A few guests mingled nearby the almost-empty spread, including a blond woman who was—or wasn't—the same one Sadie had seen that afternoon at Bertie's Beach Baubles. Minus the baseball cap, sunglasses, and casual beachwear, it was difficult to tell. Dressed in an elegant peach-colored linen shift, soft multipastel-colored shawl, and strappy heels, she might well be someone else. But one thing was certain: if it was the same person, her expression was far from the cheerful one she'd sported at the boardwalk boutique.

Returning to join Myrtle, Sadie shared those thoughts. "There's something about that blond woman over there that's bothering me."

"Which one? There must be forty blond women in this room." Myrtle followed Sadie's gaze. "The one talking to the man facing away from us?"

"Yes," Sadie said. "I think I saw her in that accessory shop on the boardwalk today. The one I picked this up at." She fingered the flip-flop necklace absentmindedly, noting the woman did not have the same one on, which would have confirmed her suspicions.

"I recognize her," Myrtle said.

"You do?" Sadie looked at Myrtle. "You know her?"

Myrtle shook her head immediately. "No, I don't know her. I don't know anyone here. Except you now," she added. "But I'm pretty sure that's the woman who hurried out of the room after the announcement that GQ would not be able to make the dinner."

Sadie thought that over. She hadn't paid a lot of attention to other guests at the front table, but she did remember a woman was one of several who stood and left right away, all appearing to be upset. "You might be right. Maybe I know a way we can find out who it is…"

"Your detective beau in New Orleans?" Myrtle smiled.

"I wouldn't call him a beau." Sadie blushed in spite of attempts not to. "I'd say a good friend with beau potential. Anyway, I have an easier source. Just a minute." She slipped her cell phone out of her tote bag, patting Coco on the head in the process just to give the Yorkie some overdue attention. Between the food and the crowd, the petite canine was spending a lot of time inside the tote.

Moving across the room, Sadie made a point of taking a few photos of paintings, statues, and other miscellaneous items. Slowly and discreetly nearing the blond woman, she angled the phone in the opposite direction, and then clicked the reverse view so it would take a picture over her shoulder. Checking the results, she smiled and returned to Myrtle.

"Okay," Myrtle said. "Now what?"

"We send it to my best source for showbiz information." Sadie opened a text message to Amber and sent the photo through, followed with a question about identifying the blond woman. "Now we just wait for an answer. She may be with customers, so it might be a little while."

It only took a few seconds to get a response.

How did you get that picture of Kira Fairchild?

Sadie and Myrtle exchanged glances "Who?" they each mouthed to the other. Sadie typed the question back to Amber.

She's part of GQ's entourage, an assistant with makeup and wardrobe. Some people think she's his girlfriend, but he always denies it. There was a pause, and then Amber sent a correction. *Denied it. He always denied it.*

What do you think? Sadie typed and hit Send. She could almost see Amber shrug her shoulders through the phone.

Who knows? It doesn't matter now, does it? Another pause followed. *Customer entering.*

Sadie said a quick goodbye and let Amber get back to business.

"Find anything out?" Myrtle asked after Sadie slid the phone back into the tote bag.

"Maybe, maybe not," Sadie said. "Apparently, there were rumors about GQ having a girlfriend, specifically the blonde over there."

Myrtle's mouth dropped open. "Really? Wasn't he voted Sexiest Eligible Bachelor in that celebrity magazine last year?"

Sadie shrugged her shoulders. "You'd have to ask Amber. I don't follow that stuff."

"Right," Myrtle said. "Well, I'm sure he was. I remember seeing it on the magazine cover."

"That means…" Sadie tapped one finger against her lips, thinking. "It would be good business to keep a girlfriend a secret. What lovestruck fan wants to feel she doesn't have a chance?"

Myrtle nodded. "That's a good point."

"Yes," Sadie said. "It's a very good point indeed."

NINE

Sadie returned to her room after bidding Myrtle goodbye. She opened the door to the private patio and let Coco run around while she leaned back in a lounge chair. A cool breeze had started up, bringing a sense of levity, as if the light wind would allow normal breathing to resume. After the emotions and stress of the past twenty-four hours, it was a welcome feeling, whether imagined or not.

On a whim, Sadie had ordered room service without realizing she was full from indulging in appetizers. She'd signed for the club sandwich and side order of fruit when it arrived, tipped the bellman, and slid the food in the suite's refrigerator for later. The chilled glass of chardonnay that accompanied the meal was welcome, however. It now graced the small patio table beside her, a seashell-design, mosaic-tiled coaster below it.

The early evening scene on the beach stood out in sharp contrast to the hectic activity the previous night. The weather channel had predicted rain on approach, but none had arrived yet. In spite of gray clouds gathering above, the activity along the shore seemed calm and casual. Yellow police tape had been removed, and beachgoers strolled along the sand just as if a dead body hadn't been there less than twenty-four hours before. In all likelihood, some weren't even aware of the tragic event. A young couple walked along the water's edge, hand in hand. A small boy and a man tossed a beach ball back and forth. Two surfers paddled outward from the shore, preparing to catch a few waves before either rain or the setting sun prevented it.

Sadie closed her eyes for a moment, pulling a sweater around her shoulders and enjoying the wisps of cool air blowing across her face. This was a particular balance she'd grown to love over the years, wrapping herself in something warm and comforting while allowing a cooler contrast of temperature on her face.

Tempted to doze, her eyes fluttered open when something hard and cold hit her foot. Glancing down, she noted a seashell, covered with sand. It rested above her big toe and extended sideways two toes over. A smiling, panting Coco stood over it, looking up at Sadie proudly.

"Very nice, Coco," Sadie said as she picked up the seashell and set it next to her drink's coaster, too comfortable to stand and add it to a pile of similar shells that Coco had hunted down the day before. "I see you've been off on one of your scavenger hunts." This was a favorite pastime for the petite canine. A basket of collected treasures graced the floor of Sadie's San Francisco penthouse, some of them gathered on trips, others simply pulled at random from around the apartment. Anytime Sadie couldn't find something—at least something small enough to fit between the Yorkie's teeth—the basket was the first place she looked. Bracelets, phone messages, socks, even kitchen towels were at risk of joining the collection. It never seemed to bother Coco when Sadie retrieved items; she simply trotted off to round up replacements.

A double buzz from Sadie's cell phone alerted her to an incoming text. She scooped Coco up into her lap to keep her from running off again and then picked up the phone.

Ms. Kramer.

Detective Broussard.

Relaxing yet?

Sadie had to think before responding. Yes, she was relaxing, although she was certain that wasn't Broussard's underlying question. He'd be concerned that she'd become further embroiled in the mystery at hand instead of enjoying the seaside vacation she was supposed to be on.

Yes, Sadie replied. It was a truthful statement, after all. How else would one interpret sitting on a beachside patio lounge chair, sipping wine and feeling the evening breeze? She was certainly relaxing. At least her body was. Her mind still replayed scenes and conversations she'd witnessed during the past twenty-four hours. *Enjoying some quiet time on the patio's lounge chair*, she added.

Evening plans?

Sadie smiled, choosing to think he might be feeling a tinge of jealousy though she suspected it was merely light conversation.

Pajamas, wine, and reading, Sadie answered. *I picked up a new mystery. I can't resist bookracks at airports.*

She laughed out loud after sending the text and rereading it on the screen. Both statements were true individually as well as together. She had picked up a paperback in the airport gift shop. But she'd obviously also picked up a new mystery unrelated to the book.

Sadie took a sip of wine and looked out at the beach. The man and young boy were departing, the older of the two holding the boy's hand while cradling the beach ball under his other arm. The couple had moved on, no longer in sight. The surfers continued to battle the waves. She suspected they would be the last to come in, likely after raindrops started to fall.

———

"And you, Detective Broussard," Sadie typed. *"Exciting evening plans?"* Two could play at this game, naturally.

Yes, if you consider filling out reports on three related burglaries to be exciting.

Sadie selected confetti emojis from the phone options and clicked Send. *I'm truly jealous,* she added. *At least you're getting to solve crimes.* She winced after sending the last line, knowing what would soon follow on his end.

Speaking of which…

Yep, just as she expected. She stretched back in the lounge chair and waited for the rest.

How is that situation going there at the hotel?

Sadie sighed, wishing she had exciting inside information to relay. But the truth was, she didn't. Whatever developments there were could already be found on national broadcasts or on the internet. *Nothing much to report,* she typed. *Only what's already on the news.*

Feeling the wind shift in that unique pre-thunderstorm way, Sadie stood and picked up her wineglass. With her cell phone in one hand and the chardonnay in the other, she used her elbow to maneuver the handle of the sliding glass door and, calling Coco to follow, moved inside.

I've made a new friend, Sadie typed after getting settled in an overstuffed armchair. *Myrtle,* she added. Not that it was necessary to clarify that it wasn't a male friend. She and the New Orleans detective hadn't specifically defined their relationship as more than friendship. However, he *had* sent her roses the previous Valentine's Day. It seemed only fair to not leave the announcement open to interpretation.

Aha. Is she as crazy as you?

Sadie rolled this last text around in her mind, contemplating the possible insinuations. Deciding to take it as a compliment, she smiled and responded. *Maybe not quite, but not everyone is perfect.* She mentally patted herself on the back for her snarky reply and took a sip of wine to celebrate her cleverness. In fact, it was quite possible that Myrtle was as eccentric as Sadie herself, in which case they made a perfect pair. It was a double bonus to her vacation, finding both a mystery and a kindred spirit.

"Coco, no," Sadie said aloud, realizing she'd made a mistake leaving the sliding glass door partially open. It was her own fault that a slimy piece of kelp now adorned one of her bare feet. If she had wanted an ankle bracelet, she could have picked one up at Bertie's Beach Baubles. A dry one, even. And Coco herself was a bit on the drippy side, an indication that rain had now joined the wind outside.

BRB. Coco is collecting souvenirs that I need to return to their rightful place. Sadie set the phone down and grasped the kelp between one thumb and forefinger. She walked back to the patio and flung it out on the sand as a rumble of thunder sounded overhead. She retreated inside, making sure the door to the patio was closed securely on her way back in.

A miniature criminal? Broussard had texted while she was disposing of the undesirable item.

Just beach debris, Sadie typed. *I don't think that counts.*

In that case, no charges will be filed.

Sadie laughed out loud. She appreciated an officer of the law with a good sense of humor. *I'd better get the little rascal settled down for the night.*

Yes. Before the situation escalates and she becomes a jewel thief.

Again, Sadie chuckled. *Enjoy your reports!*

Ending the text exchange, Sadie set her phone down, dried Coco off with a towel, and escorted the Yorkie to her travel palace. Bending down to latch the door to the luxury kennel, she whispered, "We just won't tell him about the time you retrieved that diamond bracelet at a banquet, okay?"

With a yip of gratitude, Coco curled up on her velvet cushion and yawned. Taking this as a brilliant suggestion, Sadie changed into her pink flamingo pajamas, fluffed the pillows on the hotel bed, and followed suit. Three pages into the mystery novel she'd picked up at the airport, she fell asleep to the sound of rain beating against the sliding glass doors.

TEN

Sadie sat up and stretched her arms above her head. Sunlight flowed in from the patio, a welcome sight after listening to the storm throughout the night. Pelting rain and howling wind had interrupted Sadie's slumber more than once, though she never found it difficult to go back to sleep.

"Looks like the weather has cleared up," Sadie said as she leaned down and unlatched the travel palace's door. In an almost similar motion to that of Sadie, Coco lifted her head from the velvet beneath her and stretched all four legs. Sufficiently invigorated, she trotted to the patio door and waited to be let out for her morning constitutional.

Sadie opened the sliding glass door enough to let Coco escape to the patio garden, and then she headed to the room's coffee maker. *These newfangled cup contraptions!* Sadie thought to herself as she pondered the unfamiliar machine. Personally, she was fond of the old-style model she had at home. Other than replacing the glass pot a couple of times over the years, it had always been steadfast in service.

With coffee finally brewing, Sadie returned to the sitting area where she found Coco sitting up straight, waiting. A sandy twig of driftwood lay on a section of tile floor in front of the dog.

"What have you fetched this time?" Coco tilted her head to the side as Sadie picked up the driftwood by one end and took a closer look. She shook the piece of wood lightly, and a metallic clinking sound followed. Reaching back down to the floor, she retrieved a chain with a small, round pendant attached. Somewhat worn and encrusted with sand, Sadie still knew immediately what it was.

"You found a St. Christopher medal, Coco." She held the pendant in the air and let the necklace swing back and forth. Coco's fuzzy head swayed side to side as it followed the motion. "St. Christopher is the patron saint of travelers. We used to wear these back in school," Sadie explained. "I'm not sure if we really thought it would keep us safe while traveling or if we just thought it made us look cool. But they were very popular." Coco sat up even straighter, certain this was one of her finer catches.

Sadie carried the pendant to the bathroom sink, rinsed it off, and inspected both sides. The back of the medal appeared to have been engraved at some point, but the inscription was too worn to read.

"We'll check with the front desk to see if anyone lost this," Sadie said. She set the necklace aside and wrapped her hand around the handle of a now-ready cup of coffee. Grateful that the caffeine infusion could begin, she carried the steaming mug to the patio and sent a text to Myrtle.

Good morning!

It only took a minute to get a reply. *The same to you. Coffee?*

Having some now in the room but can meet up. It didn't matter that she had mastered the coffee maker and already held a cup. Meeting for coffee was just an excuse to get together in the same way someone might say "Let's do lunch." Besides, she'd spotted some delicious-looking scones in the display case of the hotel's coffee bar the day before.

The lobby in fifteen, Myrtle suggested via another quick text.

Sounds good. Sadie sent the reply, set her phone aside, and took a generous gulp of coffee. She moved to the closet and perused her clothing options for the morning, which only served to remind her of the need to check out additional shops along the boardwalk. What would a vacation be without a few new purchases to take home? She had the necklaces from Bertie's, but that was hardly enough. While she was shopping, she could stop in at the surf shop. Perhaps they might know if one of the regular surfers had lost a pendant—a St. Christopher pendant, to be precise.

Sadie clicked hanger after hanger together, debating an outfit for the morning. Finally choosing navy slacks and a nautical-themed top, she frowned at the blasé image in the mirror. It looked frumpy in spite of the silver-sequined anchor applique on the front of the blouse. She shrugged her shoulders and headed for the lobby, terrier-laden tote in tow. *All the more reason to go shopping.*

Myrtle was easy to spot, having dressed more to Sadie's usual standards. Her bright neon-orange tunic stood out among the more typical attire at other tables in the coffee bar area. A flowery hat that would live up to Kentucky Derby standards hung on the back of her chair.

"You must have read my mind!" Sadie exclaimed as she joined Myrtle. Two raspberry scones waited on crisp wax paper doilies alongside beverages that matched their individual choices the morning before. She slid into a seat, eyeing the scones with eager anticipation.

"Well, dig in then," Myrtle said, reaching for one of the freshly baked scones herself, "so that I can do the same. Calories love company, I always say."

Sadie nodded with approval. "I like that philosophy."

"Works for pizza too," Myrtle quipped.

"Anything new this morning?" Sadie looked around the

lobby as if that might give her an answer. Seeing nothing but normal hotel activity, she turned back to Myrtle, who shook her head.

"Same old, same old," Myrtle said. "Nothing new on the morning news either. Perhaps that's all there is, what we already know."

Sadie looked at Myrtle, both eyebrows raised. "Really? A celebrity washes up on the beach and that's the end of the story? I don't think so. Even the lack of additional news is news to me."

"I bet GQ's manager is just keeping things quiet," Myrtle suggested. "Out of respect."

"Because Hollywood is so well known for respect and privacy?" Sadie couldn't resist pointing out the obvious.

"Good point," Myrtle said.

"I'm sure it was difficult for Mr. Chalinder—that's his name, right? GQ's personal manager?" Myrtle nodded in response to Sadie's question. "Difficult for Mr. Chalinder to identify the body." Sadie continued. "He might not be ready to make any other statements at this time. But…"

"But what?"

"I don't buy that," Sadie said. "It's his job to handle the press. I don't think his personal feelings would get in the way. And the police could issue statements without his permission. I suspect we'll hear something else later today."

"Or even now," Myrtle said. She nodded toward a newspaper stand in the front lobby where a hotel worker was restocking copies of the morning's publication.

"Good eye," Sadie said. "I tried to grab a copy on the way down from my room, but the rack was empty." She took another bite of raspberry scone while standing up, causing a few crumbs to flutter down. Brushing them off the tabletop, she crossed the lobby and grabbed a copy of the paper, then returned to her chair.

"Already not front-page news?" Myrtle quirked an eyebrow as she glanced at the paper Sadie set down. "I doubt GQ would like being upstaged by politics. He never liked being upstaged by anything."

"No, it's still front page," Sadie said, having unfolded the newspaper. "See?" She pointed to an article on the lower half of the paper. The headline, though not as large as the one for the newest Washington, DC, scandal above it, still boldly proclaimed "Quinlan Death Investigation Ongoing."

"Anything new?" Myrtle leaned forward as Sadie skimmed the article.

"Nothing, really," Sadie said. "It says that no conclusions have been drawn about how he ended up in the ocean." She tapped her fingers on the table while reading on. "And… wait, there is something." She turned the paper toward Myrtle and pointed to one line.

Interviews at the Casa Playa hotel have led to a possible person of interest, but the police have not released any specific information, and no arrests have been made.

"What do you make of that?" Myrtle said. "Those officers didn't spend much time with people here in the lobby yesterday morning."

"No," Sadie agreed. "But they were milling around casually at the appetizer hour. Or, I imagine, not as casually as they appeared to be. They must have found something out. Or at least something that struck them as suspicious."

"Any other information?" Myrtle took a sip of coffee while Sadie continued to scan the page.

"Only some contradictory details," Sadie said. "The technical cause of death is listed as drowning."

"So then it was an accident?" Myrtle said. "That's what it sounds like to me."

"Then why would they have a person of interest?" Sadie pointed out. "And it also mentions blunt force trauma, possibly with something heavy but not sharp. You see how this sounds contradictory?"

Myrtle shrugged her shoulders. "Not really. I don't think 'person of interest' implies a suspect necessarily. It's just someone they think might have more information. Like how GQ ended up in the ocean to begin with."

"Which is in itself a good question," Sadie said. "How *did* he end up in the ocean?"

ELEVEN

Sadie ran her finger along a rack of brightly patterned clothing, selecting some new pieces of beachwear while ruminating on the variety of ways a body might end up in the Pacific Ocean. She pulled out a yellow sundress with a colorful starfish design and tossed it over one arm while questioning whether GQ might have simply gone out for a swim and drowned. However, that didn't explain the blunt force trauma mentioned in the paper. Had he been hit by an object floating in the water?

While adding a tent-shaped cover-up with horizontal stripes, Sadie debated whether he might have gotten caught in a riptide. As she plucked a wraparound sarong with a palm tree print from another rack, she also considered the possibility that the much-loved celebrity might have attempted surfing without adequate experience. Perhaps the surfboard hit him and knocked him out. Yet no wayward surfboard had been found. If so, surely that would have been in the news already.

"Would you like me to put those in a dressing room for you?"

The voice jolted Sadie out of her thoughts, and she turned toward a young sales clerk dressed in ripped cutoff jeans, a white T-shirt, and sandals. The outfit struck Sadie as oddly bland for a shop filled with rich colors and unique designs.

"I'll be happy to hold those for you." The salesgirl reached out for Sadie's selections. Her smile hovered above a name tag that said Maya.

Realizing she had yet to reply, Sadie thanked the girl and simply asked where the dressing room was located. Following Maya's extended arm, Sadie strolled to the back of the shop, hung her choices on a wall peg, and pulled the dressing room curtain closed. She set down her tote bag and lifted Coco out, letting the Yorkie sit on a built-in bench.

"This way you can give me your opinion, Coco," Sadie said. She patted the petite canine on the head and proceeded to change into the yellow sundress. That is, she attempted to. "When did clothing get this small?" she asked Coco, who had the good sense not to respond at all. "Oh well." She replaced the dress on a hanger and tried on the tent-shaped cover-up. But the loose cut of the style combined with the horizontal stripes was anything but slimming. Sighing, she replaced that one on the hanger as well and added it to the go-back pile.

Unsure at this point that anything would please her—some shopping days were just like that, after all—she tried on the sarong. Her eyes lit up. The casual wraparound style was forgiving enough to accept her hips' curves, and the longer-than-knee-length hemline allowed her to feel she wasn't trying to dress thirty years younger than she actually was.

"Aha, Coco!" she exclaimed. "I think we have a winner. What do you think?" Coco tilted her head to one side, then the other, and offered a yip of approval, earning herself a pat on the head.

Sadie changed back into her own clothing, helped Coco settle back into the tote bag, and draped the sarong over her arm. As she pulled back the curtain to exit, she noticed a small advertisement on the dressing room wall.

The words Cappy's Coastal Cruises ran across the top of the ad, followed by a photograph of a sightseeing boat on the water. Several passengers relaxed by the rails of the small vessel. A new theory began to form in Sadie's head. She could hardly wait to discuss it with Myrtle as well as with Broussard.

"Are those boat tours popular?" Sadie asked Maya as the salesgirl rang up the sarong.

"Boat tours?"

"Like the ad on the dressing room wall," Sadie explained, realizing her question had come out of nowhere. She'd never been good about making sure to include a frame of reference when excited.

"Oh, those," Maya said. "I guess they are. I hear a lot of people talk about them." She wrapped the sarong in tissue and slipped it into a handled paper bag with a store logo sticker on it.

"Is their office near here?" Sadie asked.

"Whose office?" Maya handed over the bag, obviously confused.

"Cappy's," Sadie said. "I think that's what your ad says in the dressing room."

"Now I understand," Maya said. "I didn't know what you meant by Cappy's. We don't handle those ads, so I don't pay attention to them. It's just a company that comes around and changes them every month. I guess businesses can sign up for paid promotion."

Sadie nodded. "Got it. How about another office nearby? Maybe a different company that offers boat trips for tourists?"

"Not really," Maya said, shaking her head. "Most of those tours come out of Long Beach or San Pedro. Not locally."

"I see," Sadie said, considering the geography of the California coast. "So, north of here."

Maya nodded.

"Thank you," Sadie said, smiling. "You've been very helpful.

And I love the sarong! I may just come back for another one in a different color."

Sadie continued along the boardwalk, reluctantly passing other beachwear shops that tempted her inside. Noting the names of those most appealing so she could return, she headed directly to the surf shop where she found the same young surfer working the last time she'd stopped by. He recognized her right away, which saved the effort of introducing herself all over again.

"Back to sign up for surf lessons this time?" A not-unkind snicker accompanied the remark.

"I'm thinking about it," Sadie said, knowing he wouldn't take her answer any more seriously than his own question had been. "I really just came by to let you know a St. Christopher medal washed up on the beach near the hotel. I thought one of your regular customers might mention losing one. There were a couple of surfers out there last night. Maybe it belonged to one of them?"

A shrug was the response. "Who knows? Stuff washes up on the beach all the time."

"That's pretty much what I figured," Sadie said. It hadn't hurt to ask. She moved on to a more important question. "I also wanted to check something you told me last time I was here, about the direction of the currents."

The surfer nodded. "North to south. Here, I'll give you a map of the currents." He retreated into the surf shack and emerged with a single piece of paper. "This shows the patterns along the coast here, plus some farther out to sea."

Sadie took the paper, impressed with the swirling lines and arrows. "Yes, I see it's pretty clear. I'm sure I learned about this in school but just didn't remember." Coco, hearing paper crinkling, stuck her head out of the tote bag and inspected the paper as well.

"You'd remember if you were out there riding the waves. There's more to surfing than just jumping in the ocean and having fun." The young man held one hand over his forehead and looked out toward the water. "The ocean currents, weather patterns, wind—all of that makes a difference. Safety, you know?" He dropped his hand and gave Coco a pat on the head.

Sadie thanked him for the map, which she slid inside her tote. She started back to the hotel but then retraced her steps to hit a couple of the beach shops she'd noted earlier. Three hours, two souvenir T-shirts, one flowing skirt with a seashell print, one floppy beach hat, three enameled mermaid brooches, and four surfboard key chains later, she returned to her suite.

"An impressive haul, if I do say so myself," she clucked as she surveyed the spread of purchases. The skirt was an especially exciting find. The beige, mocha and sienna tones of the seashells against a swirling blue and aqua background would match several blouses she had back in San Francisco. And her favorite pair of gold metallic flats would complete the outfit. She sighed, wishing she'd brought those with her on this trip. They'd be perfect to wear to the evening appetizer hour.

Thinking of the mini-taquitos from the night before, Sadie checked the room clock, delighted to find it was already time to head to the lobby. Her excursion along the boardwalk had served to build up her appetite. Excited to see what treats would be at the buffet this time, she changed from the drab nautical outfit she'd been wearing to leopard-print leggings and a brown rayon blouse with a silver-studded collar. Not to leave Coco out of the fashion show, she switched the Yorkie's usual rhinestone collar for one that matched her leggings. The leopard print looked exotic against Coco's fur. She could almost imagine Coco as a wild jungle animal. Well, almost.

When Sadie reached the lobby, Myrtle already had a table staked out with a plate of the hotel's appetizers for the evening.

"I had a feeling you'd show up here," Myrtle said, indicating the chair beside her.

Sadie sat down and grabbed a miniature quiche. Secretively—even if only for dramatic effect—she leaned in close and pulled the map of ocean currents out of her tote, which took a few pulls and word of reprimand, as Coco held on to it like the ferocious wild animal she must have now thought she was.

"Wait until you hear my theory," Sadie whispered.

Myrtle raised her eyebrows. "Theory?"

Sadie spread the map out on the table and pointed to the arrows along the California coast.

"I don't understand." Myrtle popped a quiche into her mouth and waited for an explanation.

"These are the ocean currents," Sadie said. "The guy at the surf shop gave me the map."

"You went back to that surf shop?" Myrtle looked worried. "You aren't going to take up surfing, are you? I have a cousin who tried to do that in her late fifties. Now the pins in her leg always set off the security system when she flies."

"Of course not," Sadie said, somewhat dismayed that everyone seemed to think she was too old to take up an active sport. Granted, surfing might be a bit extreme, but she wasn't ready to limit herself to bridge games and checkers.

"So the ocean currents have given you a theory? No offense, Sadie," Myrtle said, taking a close look at the map. "But we already know the body came out of the ocean. And everyone knows the currents flow north to south."

Everyone except me, apparently. Sadie frowned and then spoke up. "That's only part of it. It's an ad on a dressing room wall that gave me the idea."

"What kind of ad? And… what dressing room?" Myrtle's eyes brightened. "What did you buy?"

"A sarong, but that's beside the point. The ad was for *boat* tours."

"Boat tours," Myrtle repeated. "And you think…"

Sadie nodded. "I think Garrison Quinlan went out on a boat tour the afternoon of the dinner. Or maybe in the morning. It doesn't matter. What matters is…"

"…he didn't come back on the boat," Myrtle said.

"Exactly!" Sadie said triumphantly. "Now we just have to figure out…"

"…why he went, who he went with, when he went, and how he ended up on the beach here instead of returning on the boat and then coming to the dinner to be the guest of honor."

"Right," Sadie confirmed.

"Just why, who, when, and how," Myrtle said. "That's all we need to figure out?"

"Yeah… that's all." Sadie's enthusiasm dimmed as the weakness of her theory became clear.

"So what now?"

Sadie sighed. "Let's find out if this theory of mine is anything but rubbish."

TWELVE

"Hello, is this Sid's Seaside Sailing? I'm Sally Ann Kranger from the *Winnemucca Post*. I understand Garrison Quinlan was on a boat tour of yours recently."

It was a lie, of course, but only partially, Sadie rationalized. She might be fibbing about her identity and employer, but she was wondering if the deceased celebrity had been on the company's boat tour. And the outfit she'd called before that, Otto's Outboard Outfitters. And the other eighteen tour operators she'd contacted. Arnie's Aquatic Adventures had directed her to Manny's Marine Motorboats, who had sent her to Ernie's Excellent Expeditions. So far, no bites. She figured if she scored the right vendor, at least she'd get a moment of hesitation before they denied it. And deny it they would, naturally. Who'd want to admit to the press that they'd lost a passenger? It would hardly be good for business.

The call to Sid's Seaside Sailing simply led to a dead end. A receptionist—an oddity in the boat rental business as far as Sadie was concerned—transferred her to a reservation service, which took a message. Several other calls had gone to voice mail directly, including the first one she'd made to Cappy's. She wasn't getting anywhere, yet she continued to try.

A ringtone accompanying Amber's name on her cell phone interrupted what felt like a fruitless and never-ending search.

Gladly disconnecting from Tony's Tidal Tours, which had kept her on hold listening to Frankie Ford's recording of *Sea Cruise* over and over, she answered the incoming call.

"Amber, good to hear from you," Sadie said. "Everything okay at the store?"

"Yeah, no problems, it's been a quiet morning," Amber said. "I sold a pair of those rhinestone sunglasses you like, also a silk scarf. And Mrs. Thomas picked up the sweater she ordered last week. That's about it."

"Well, getting a few sales is better than no sales at all," Sadie said. "Maybe it'll pick up later. Did Matteo bring over any new truffles?" Just the thought of the magnificent confections at Cioccolato, next door to the boutique, made her long for home.

Amber laughed. "Yes, as a matter of fact. He made a batch of mango pecan truffles with drizzles of dark chocolate. Delicious."

"And you're saving me one, right? Maybe… two?" A thrill of anticipation ran through Sadie just thinking about it.

"Naturally," Amber said. "But that's not why I'm calling you. Some rumors are floating around on the internet about GQ's…"

Sadie knew why Amber was having trouble finishing the sentence. Death was rarely an easy word to say.

"Oh!" Sadie exclaimed. "I've been on the phone for, well, way too long, so I haven't checked for updates anywhere. Tell me."

"They're saying there might have been high levels of alcohol and some kind of drug in GQ's…"

Amber's voice trailed off again, which Sadie understood. The word *body* wasn't any easier than the word *death*. And the two combined made for depressing conversation.

"But it can't be true!" Amber said. "He went to rehab years ago and has been clean ever since!"

"What kind of problems sent him to rehab?" Sadie asked. She ran a few combinations through her mind that she knew could be disastrous if combined with alcohol—benzodiazepines, opioids, even stimulants.

"Hydrocodone, I think," Amber said. "Or maybe it was Vicodin. Something like that."

Prescription opioids, Sadie mused. It could be another sad accidental overdose case, far too common. Or was it?

Amber must have been reading her mind, as her next comment was, "It doesn't make sense, Sadie. GQ was active with drug prevention programs. He spoke at schools and rehab centers, and he did those public service announcements on TV."

"Maybe he had a problem that no one knew about," Sadie suggested even though she knew it wouldn't be what Amber wanted to hear. "Some people relapse."

"I don't want to believe it!" Amber said.

Yep, called that one right, Sadie thought to herself.

"And," Amber continued, "how did he end up in the water? He was terrified of water. It was a phobia going back to childhood. Everyone knows that."

Not everyone, Sadie thought, counting herself among the least knowledgeable about pop culture and that sort of thing.

"Wouldn't he have passed out wherever he was?" Amber continued. "Do you think he could have been so out of it that he decided to go swimming without knowing how? I mean, actually swim out far enough to drown?"

Sadie resisted the impulse to point out that someone could drown in very little water. It wouldn't help. As it was, she had the urge to reach through the phone and hug Amber to comfort her. She hadn't heard her shop manager this upset in a long time, and she understood. Garrison Quinlan had been Amber's biggest celebrity crush.

"I'm not sure," Sadie admitted. "I don't know much about drug combinations. Maybe he took something right before entering the water. He would have still felt okay going in." Sadie's new theory ran through her mind, but she thought it better not to further upset Amber with the additional possibilities of a boat tour and head or bodily trauma. Besides, the boat idea was nothing more than a hunch at this point.

Amber sighed. "I'm going to eat another truffle and then go inventory the scarves. I'll make notes of which ones we need to reorder."

"Good idea," Sadie said. "You can even have the truffle you were going to save for me."

"Oh, no, no, no," Amber said. "I know better than to come between you and your chocolate. Don't worry. Yours will be sitting on your desk when you get back."

Sadie laughed. "Then treat yourself to more from next door if needed. Take it out of petty cash. That's exactly what the petty cash is for: emergencies."

"The need for chocolate being an emergency," Amber said.

"I see I've trained you well." Saying goodbye, Sadie let Amber get on with the shop tasks. Without even setting the phone down, she immediately sent off a text to Myrtle.

Possible new info, Sadie typed.

Already saw the rumors online. Nothing confirmed. What do you think?

Sadie held her fingers over the phone's keyboard, contemplating the answer to Myrtle's question. What *did* she think? An alcohol and drug combination could have contributed to GQ's death, but it didn't lead to any conclusions. Was it a self-inflicted overdose, a result of the personal problems Amber had first told her about? Or was it an accident, maybe a little partying carried too far? Or was it something more sinister? Foul play and all that.

It's not much to go on.

Agreed, Myrtle sent back. *There's no official statement saying it was the cause of death.*

Has the news said what the cause was? Or speculated? Sadie shook her head. Why hadn't she thought to ask Amber if she'd heard anything about that?

Based on a vague statement from an anonymous source, they're now debating accidental drowning from blunt force trauma. There's no official report from the medical examiner yet.

Sadie pondered that. How would a person die accidentally from blunt force trauma? It was possible he might have fallen, hit his head on something, and been knocked unconscious. But how would that happen on a beach? And why would he then end up in the water? It didn't add up.

A sharp yip from Coco drew Sadie's eyes up from the phone. Knowing Coco's expressions well, Sadie knew she was being reprimanded, and she deserved it. Between phone calls and texts, she'd barely given the Yorkie a glance all morning. She sent a quick text to Myrtle to let her know she'd catch up to her later. The responsibilities of dog ownership called.

"How about your pink rhinestone collar and leash?" Sadie asked, holding the items up for Coco to inspect. Not hearing a vote of disapproval—Coco was prone to the occasional whine—Sadie attached the sparkling items. She clipped a pink bow on top of Coco's head for a finishing touch, and they headed out for a walk.

The beach reflected the usual scene—young women stretching out on colorful beach towels in hopes of acquiring tans, older women reading books while seated in portable folding chairs and wearing hats to shade their faces, children digging into the sand with plastic shovels and buckets. And, of course, the tumbling waves, polka-dotted with surfers.

Coco, ecstatic to be out amid the action, trotted along beside Sadie while yipping hello to anyone passing by. Especially pleased with those who stopped to pet her head, she'd licked more than one sandaled foot by the time Sadie tugged her leash gently and led her over to a beachside café. After being served a glass of water—"for you, ma'am"—and a bowl of water—"for the little darling"—Sadie ordered a basket of fish and chips and sat back to people-watch, a favorite activity.

"Look, that woman sitting on the boardwalk bench is wearing my sarong," Sadie said. "I think that's the same woman we keep seeing—Kira Fairchild." She scooped Coco up into her lap. "Well, obviously, it's not my sarong she's wearing, but I bet it's from the same shop." That served as a reminder to go back and pick up another. She'd found it to be a good shopping practice to buy two of something she knew would be a favorite piece of clothing. It never seemed possible to find the same item again later on.

The basket of crisp, battered fish and hot, salty fries landed on the table, along with a pleated paper cup of tartar sauce and a bottle of vinegar. Coco craned her petite neck, far more interested in the basket's contents than the sarong Sadie had pointed out. Not oblivious to Coco's tricks, Sadie pushed the food away from the edge of the table, picked up a fry, and waved it in the air to cool it down. Holding it in front of Coco's mouth, she let the Yorkie take a nibble.

Sadie added several generous splashes of vinegar to the fish, dipped a piece into the sauce, and took a bite. She closed her eyes and sighed. There was nothing like good old fried food, healthy or not. And, being on vacation, she reminded herself it was calorie-free.

Opening her eyes, her attention was drawn back to the woman across the way, certain now that it was Kira Fairchild. This time it wasn't the colorful sarong that caught Sadie's eye but a man sliding onto the bench beside her. He slipped his arm around the woman's waist in an oddly casual manner that almost appeared secretive. A baseball cap shaded his face, making it difficult to discern his features. But a brief gust of wind provided all the information Sadie needed. In the time it took him to grab his cap and replace it on his head, it was clear the man was none other than James Chalinder.

THIRTEEN

Sadie returned to the hotel after lunch with a doggie bag of leftover fish and chips plus two more shopping bags. One held the extra sarong she'd picked up, the other, an ankle-length yellow shift with a conservative slit up the side and a school of smiling fish embroidered around the neckline. She added both to the growing collection of beachwear in her closet and then moved to the sitting area of the suite.

It was only on rare occasion that Sadie opened her laptop while on vacation, but she always made a point of having it with her. After getting Coco occupied nearby with a chew toy, she fired the computer up and proceeded to search every celebrity website that she could find. Shocked at how much information came up—some possibly accurate, much probably not—she absorbed one trashy detail after another, trying to sort out fact from fiction. There were enough photos online to fill any fan's scrapbook—red carpet poses, celebrity golf tournaments, charity events, even still shots from filming locations. In addition, there were pictures of GQ as a child, as a young teen, as a high school quarterback, and as the heartthrob adult who constantly graced magazine covers today.

After observing Kira Fairchild and James Chalinder together on the boardwalk, she'd grown curious about what role the woman really played in Garrison Quinlan's life. Perhaps she played no role at all and the secret love interest rumors were simply that: rumors. Photos of award events showed her standing by Mr. Chalinder's side but more in a coworker-type stance than anything romantic. This matched Sadie's observations of the two at the hotel's appetizer hour but not the closeness implied by their body language on the boardwalk.

As for Ms. Fairchild's role in relation to GQ, there weren't nearly as many photos of the two of them together, and most of them were posed group pictures. Still, a few blurry paparazzi shots told a different story, some closely matching the information Amber had told her before. One showed the couple in hooded sweatshirts and sunglasses, stepping into a limousine. Another showed Kira alone in a garden purported to be part of GQ's Bel Air estate. Was Kira Fairchild actually the star's girlfriend? Or James Chalinder's? Or neither? Or… both? Well, it was Hollywood, after all. Anything was possible.

Sadie was convinced the online information was only serving to confuse her own observations. All in all, nothing she'd seen, heard, or read that day led her any closer to figuring out how Garrison Quinlan's body ended up on the beach. She was still convinced her boat theory was the best explanation for him falling into—or being *dumped* into—the ocean, in spite of numerous companies indicating he wasn't on any of their trips.

Unless… could it have been a private rental? That would be much more difficult to track. There had to be dozens, if not hundreds, of personal boats along the shore that people were willing to rent out. He could have rented one, taken it out, slipped on a wet deck, and bumped his head. But how did he end up in the water? And how would the boat have returned to the rental location? There were too many questions and not enough answers.

Sadie pored over website after website, trying to find clues.

Finally, restless and frustrated, she closed the laptop. She scooped Coco up, got her settled in the tote bag, and headed to the lobby.

Though well before the appetizer hour, the main hotel atrium boasted a good crowd. The front desk was busy with new arrivals. A short line of guests waited to be checked in. A bellman rolled a cart in from the valet parking area, marking name tags on each piece of stacked luggage in order to deliver them to the correct room. The Beach Bum already showed some bar activity, not yet full but prepared for the buzz to follow later on. A TV behind the bar's countertop showed commentators on a sports channel.

Sadie took a seat in an extrawide armchair positioned in an ideal spot for people-watching. She set the tote bag next to her, gave Coco a pat on the head, and picked up a magazine from a side table to keep her hands busy while she took note of others in the atrium area. Two women sat on a couch across from Sadie, one speaking in animated fashion, hand gestures flying, the other nodding attentively. A distinguished-looking man with gray hair and a mustache leaned against a column. He checked his wristwatch—a Rolex, Sadie was quite sure—repeatedly, as if impatient for a room not yet ready.

A sharp popping sound caused Sadie to jump and turn her head to one side, only to see a guest had accidentally dropped a briefcase on the floor. She took a deep breath and exhaled. *Must stop watching so many crime shows late at night.* She settled against the cushioned back of the chair and watched the guest pick the briefcase up and walk away, which is when she saw, just beyond that, Kira Fairchild making a purchase in the hotel's gift shop. Not far away, James Chalinder paced back and forth, a cell phone pressed to his ear. Assuming they were together, Sadie was surprised to see Ms. Fairchild complete her transaction and walk away, passing James Chalinder as if unaware of his presence. In kind, he reacted the same way, taking no note of her passing by. In addition, he made no move to follow her.

"Well now," Sadie said, whispering into her tote bag. "Those two act like they know each other well, and then not at all. It's very peculiar."

"Are you looking for something, Ms. Kramer?"

Sadie straightened up quickly at the sound of the male voice. Expecting a stranger who simply thought talking to a tote unusual, she was surprised to see Detective Martin standing in front of her. "No. I was just having a discussion," she said.

"With your bag?" The detective's eyebrows lifted.

"Sure, why not?" Sadie quipped, simply for the amusement of not giving him a straight answer.

"I see," he said, clearly not seeing at all but not bothering to carry the ridiculous conversation further. This, Sadie understood. After all, how valuable could it possibly be to discuss why someone would talk to a bag? Secretly she was pleased that Coco chose not to yip just to add to the levity.

"I suppose you're here looking for more clues," Sadie said, stating the obvious. "Have you been able to determine if Mr. Quinlan's death was accidental or foul play?"

Detective Martin gave Sadie a mixed look of annoyance and disinterest. "You must know I can't divulge information while an investigation is ongoing."

"Well, I think it was foul play," Sadie said. Tempted to direct the statement to Coco just to further irritate the detective, she spoke to him instead.

"You do, do you?" The detective's expression remained

annoyed but now showed interest. "And why is that?" He took a seat in the closest chair and waited for an answer.

Sadie pondered her reply. She was certain GQ's death hadn't been an accident but couldn't quite pinpoint why. And a hunch wouldn't be of any use to the police, would it?

"If I recall," Detective Martin continued, "you were at the dinner as well as on the beach that night. Is that correct?"

"Yes," Sadie confirmed. "And I've been watching a couple of members of Mr. Quinlan's entourage the past two days."

"His entourage?"

"You know, the people who hang around him," Sadie said. "In particular, two who were at the dinner that night. Their behavior seemed odd to me."

"Odd in what way?"

Sadie tapped one finger against her chin, searching for the right explanation. "At times they seem close, even intimate. On other occasions, they act as if they don't even know each other. Obviously, they do, since I remember they were seated at that first table at the dinner."

"Together?" Martin asked.

Sadie thought back, trying to remember. "Not next to each other. A few seats apart, I believe."

Detective Martin nodded. "So they know each other through business then. That first table was reserved for those who worked closely with Mr. Quinlan. Manager, press liaison, agent, et cetera. It takes more than one person to handle that level of celebrity."

"Obviously," Sadie said. "But it stands to reason that some work more closely with a star than others, and the degree of association between each would be of varying levels. Look at that man with the newspaper, for example." She nodded toward James Chalinder, and the detective followed her gaze.

"What about him?"

"First, I'm certain that's Mr. Quinlan's manager. He's the one who announced that the star would not be showing up for the guest of honor appearance."

The detective remained quiet, which Sadie took to be an affirmation, though she already was sure she was right. That also meant he was the one to identify the body, a side note that she didn't see any reason to mention at the moment.

"His interactions with a blond woman who was seated at the same table have been inconsistent. Which makes me think they might be hiding something. And…" Something clicked that Sadie knew she should have recognized before. "The woman's behavior seems to vary dramatically."

Detective Martin shrugged his shoulders. "I don't find that unusual. People go through a wide range of emotions when someone they know dies."

"True," Sadie agreed. "But this strikes me as something more. When they're here in the hotel, the woman—I believe her name is Kira Fairchild—is very subdued, almost mournful."

"As would be expected of someone after the death of a friend or even acquaintance."

"Yes." Sadie agreed with Detective Martin's statement, but that only proved to strengthen her next point. "But away from here, she's cheerful, practically effervescent."

"And how exactly would you know that?" the detective asked, looking pointedly at Sadie. "You seem to be quite the amateur detective. Are you following people around? That could be considered harassment, you know."

"I am absolutely *not* following people around," Sadie said, indignant while at the same time thinking it wasn't a bad suggestion. "I simply shop a lot." She flipped an earring as if to prove her point—a point that made sense to her if not to the detective. This was clear by the puzzled look on Detective Martin's face. Sadie sighed and then continued. "I've done a fair amount of shopping on this trip, including the past two days. So I've had a chance to observe her."

"So, Ms. Fletcher, what conclusions have you drawn?"

The faint smile that accompanied Detective Martin's quipped reference to *Murder She Wrote* gave Sadie hope. At least he had a sense of humor. Maybe it would be matched with a sense of taking her observations seriously.

"My conclusion? Ms. Fairchild is hiding something."

"Really," Martin said. "And just what would that be?"

Sadie smiled her most charming smile. "I'm just the amateur, remember? You're the real detective. I suppose one of us needs to find out." *Game on.*

FOURTEEN

No sooner had Sadie returned to her hotel room and closed the door than she got her answer, courtesy of Amber. She barely caught the call by the time she set her bag down and fished out the phone.

"You won't believe this!" Amber practically shouted into the phone when Sadie answered.

"Try me," Sadie said. "Wait, one second." She kicked off her shoes and opened the door to the patio, walking outside to stretch out on a lounge chair. Coco immediately followed and curled up in the shady area below the patio's table. "Okay, go ahead."

"He's married!" Amber shouted. "Can you believe it?"

Sadie inhaled and exhaled slowly but realized immediately that the deep breathing had no real purpose. She was trying to calm Amber down, not herself.

"Married!" Amber exclaimed again.

"Oh, Amber, I'm so sorry," Sadie said, assuming her shop manager was referring to the UPS driver she'd recently begun dating. He'd seemed like such a nice guy too.

"I mean… he was married," she sputtered. "What does it matter now? This is crazy! A million women are going to feel like he cheated on them."

Whoa! Now that didn't make sense at all. San Francisco was a big city, but one driver couldn't possibly have that many customers, not on one route. Wait… *was?* She said *was* married.

"Amber, who are you talking about?"

"GQ, of course," Amber said, sniffling.

Aside from being shocked at the news herself, Sadie didn't fail to notice that the idea of GQ being married seemed even more upsetting to Amber than the idea of him being dead. Had the actual news itself not been so intriguing, she would have found it amusing. As it was, she simply wanted to know how this tied in with everything else. As a side thought, she was relieved that the UPS driver Amber had been dating was still single.

"Amber," Sadie said. "Back up. Tell me where you heard this. Is it one of those Facebook things that go around for days"—*sometimes years*, she thought to herself—"and is really just a hoax?"

"No," Amber said. "This was just on the news. An anonymous source close to GQ's lawyer leaked inside information about his will that includes a sizable amount of money going to his wife."

Sadie sighed, feeling sympathy for the unknown lawyer, whoever he or she might be. It was so hard to find trustworthy employees these days.

"And that's not all," Amber continued. "Guess who this supposed wife is?"

A double buzz interrupted the call. Looking quickly at her cell phone, Sadie saw it was a text from Myrtle, which simply said *Did you hear?* Ignoring the text for the moment, she returned to the conversation with Amber. Obviously, in the short time she'd been in the hotel lobby, she'd missed something that everyone else now seemed to know.

"You just won't believe it," Amber said. "It's Kira Fairchild!"

"What?" This time Sadie inhaled and exhaled for her own benefit. She tried to piece this information together with her most recent observations. "So she wasn't his girlfriend, even though she supposedly wasn't anyway? Instead, she was his *wife*? Again, even though she supposedly wasn't?"

"That's what they're saying." Amber sniffled into what Sadie suspected was a tissue based on the muffled sound through the phone. "And I must say you might be the only one who would phrase it that way, Sadie. It doesn't really matter. The point is he *was married!*"

"I'm sorry," Sadie said simply for Amber's sake.

"Just imagine how much money Kira Fairchild is probably going to inherit!" Amber said.

"Yes," Sadie said. "I can only imagine." *The plot thickens.*

A second text sounded from Sadie's phone. Glancing at the screen, Sadie could see it was Myrtle again. It was also closing time for Flair.

"Amber, is the shop still open?"

"Closed," Amber said. "I was just cashing out and about to vacuum."

"Good. Why don't you finish that up and then go home and rest? I have a text from Myrtle, and vacuuming will be calming for you." As Sadie expected, Amber laughed. One odd thing they agreed on was the relaxing effect of vacuuming. Whether it was the sound of the machine or the repetitive motion, it served to calm them both. Strange, but true.

After ending the call with Amber, Sadie sent a text back to Myrtle. *Yes, just heard.*

The Beach Bum. Ten minutes? Myrtle sent back.

See you there, Sadie answered.

The hotel bar was busy, but not too busy for Sadie and Myrtle to get a table in a corner where they'd have some privacy. As soon as the server—a tall, slender, tanned blond with a name tag that said Barbie—took their drink orders and walked away, they launched into a hushed conversation.

"I knew it!" Myrtle exclaimed.

"Knew what?"

"That he couldn't be the single bachelor everyone said he was," Myrtle said. "He was way too handsome. And… debonair. And…"

Sadie laughed. "And… half your age."

"Well, I have eyes, don't I?" Myrtle chuckled. "I'm not blind."

"I was on the phone with Amber when you sent the text," Sadie said. "She'd just heard the news, and she sounded devastated."

"She and half the world's population, I dare say."

"Yes…" Sadie waited while Barbie set two glasses with soda water and lime on the table, along with a bowl of salty snack mix. She signed a slip to charge the drinks to her hotel suite and popped a pretzel into her mouth. "Which tells me right there why this wasn't public knowledge."

"What do you mean?" Myrtle said. She squeezed the wedge of lime into her glass and stirred the ice and soda water around to mix in the citrus flavor.

"Would you be more inclined to choose a heartthrob who was single or married?" Sadie picked another pretzel up and tapped it against the rim of her glass for emphasis.

"Single, I suppose," Myrtle said. "All things considered. If you're going to dream about someone, it might as well be someone who's available. That way at least you can imagine you have a chance."

"Exactly!" Sadie dropped the pretzel into her tote, which caught Myrtle by surprise until Coco yipped back a thank-you. Delighted, Myrtle grabbed a second pretzel and dropped it in the bag herself. A second yip followed.

Myrtle twirled her soda water and lime around again and took a sip. "So this is about publicity."

Sadie nodded. "Yes, as for keeping his marriage a secret, that would be my guess. A married heartthrob just doesn't sell tickets as well as an eligible bachelor heartthrob does."

"Makes sense," Myrtle said.

"At least something does," Sadie mused.

"What do you mean?" Myrtle tilted her head to the side, much in the way Coco did, which caused Sadie to stifle a laugh.

"I mean it makes sense from the business side," Sadie said. "But it doesn't match what I've been observing. Kira has been somber here at the hotel."

"That doesn't surprise to me," Myrtle said. "She just lost her husband. Plus... Wait... doesn't this mean she's had to act like she *didn't* just lose her husband? Only that she's sad she lost someone she worked with? Since the marriage was secret?"

Sadie pondered that. "That's a whole lot of acting just to maintain an image that isn't going to matter anymore." She fed Coco another pretzel, whispering into the tote bag that it was the last one. "But that's not what's bothering me."

"Which is what?" Myrtle asked.

"Think about the way she's acted outside the hotel—when I saw her in Bertie's Beach Baubles, smiling and laughing," Sadie said. "Is that how you'd expect a new widow to act?"

"Of course not," Myrtle said. "Unless she was in shock."

"I don't think that's it," Sadie said. "It's like she has to play a role around people she knows, pretending to be heartbroken. But when she's away, she can drop the role. And not only that, but there's the contradictory behavior I've seen between her and the manager."

"James Chalinder, you mean. The one who announced

that GQ wouldn't be making it to dinner."

"Yes." Sadie nodded.

"That's who you think you saw her with on the boardwalk yesterday?" Myrtle asked. "On the bench? You told me about that, how close they seemed. He might have been comforting her."

Sadie leaned back in her chair and stared at Myrtle. "Do you really believe that?"

"Not really," Myrtle said. "I'm just trying to talk it all through."

"And another thing," Sadie added. "This afternoon I came down to the lobby and saw them both in the gift shop. Well, she was inside; he was outside in the hallway. They completely ignored each other, even when she made a purchase and walked away."

"You think they're trying to cover up something?" Myrtle asked.

Sadie nodded. "That's *exactly* what I'm thinking."

FIFTEEN

Sadie returned to her hotel suite with her tote bag and a bowl of salty snack mix from the Beach Bum. It wasn't theft since she fully intended to return the dish itself after enjoying its contents. She even offered snacks to a few guests as she crossed the lobby and earned a chuckle or two when Coco popped out of the tote to swipe a pretzel before disappearing again.

Back in the suite, she pulled a bottle of chilled water from the room's compact refrigerator and fired up her laptop. The new revelation that Kira Fairchild was actually Garrison Quinlan's wife put a new twist on the mystery, especially considering her recent observations about GQ's secret wife and James Chalinder. There was no question something was going on between those two.

Perhaps I should take Amber's gossip reports more seriously, Sadie thought. She hadn't paid much attention to Amber's tale about Kira Fairchild being GQ's girlfriend. Rumblings like that were common in the entertainment industry. But now that rumor made more sense. They must have been seen together enough to raise suspicion even if they were trying to hide their marriage from the public in order to protect his eligible bachelor image.

Still, Sadie was certain something was missing from the overall story. She could feel it in her gut, and her intuition was usually spot on. There was some sort of twist that everyone was overlooking. It was just a question of figuring out what it was.

She opened the cool bottle of water, took a sip, and then pulled up the photos she'd previously found, looking at them more carefully. Nothing seemed out of line with the story presented to the public. Kira and GQ stood amicably near each other in publicity shots that involved the group as a whole. There were no official pictures of the two of them together. Neither were there photos of her alone with James Chalinder.

Most images of Kira showed her by herself—on the beach in a revealing swimsuit, for example, or exiting a shop on Rodeo Drive in Beverly Hills, arms laden with shopping bags. There simply wasn't anything in print that specifically implied an involvement with either man—which meant nothing except that they were cautious and the paparazzi were obviously off their game.

Sadie moved on, searching still shots from GQ's latest hit movie. She'd always found them to be fascinating, a way of freezing time that would normally be moving forward. It allowed a different perception of a scene, as opposed to watching the film itself, where everything is continual. This was especially true in a theater where rewinding wasn't possible.

Still shots from filming locations held the most interest, and a new search turned up several additional examples. In one, GQ and a director—she assumed—stood near a bored-looking cameraman while they discussed a script the director held in his hands. In another, both cast and crew mingled around a buffet table. Sadie squinted, curious to see what the food spread contained as if she could reach into the picture and munch on something herself. A third shot showed a filming scene in which GQ and two minor cast members faced each other on blocked tape areas, director and cameraman in the foreground. A few people sat or stood off to the side.

Sadie took another swig of water and stepped away from the laptop, tilting her head from side to side to relax her neck muscles after the intensive scrutiny of the photos.

"How about a walk on the beach?" she said aloud. Just as she expected, Coco made an instant transformation from an upside-down slumber pose to a wagging-tail stance by the patio door. The magic word walk always resulted in an enthusiastic response from the Yorkie.

Sadie clipped a leash to Coco's collar and stepped out onto the patio. Delighted once again for the pet-friendly hotel and private section of beach, the two walked hand-in-leash out toward the sand. Sadie, a firm believer in responsible pet ownership, made sure the mutt-mitt container clipped to the leash had bags available before starting out. She'd always found it outrageous that people had the nerve to not clean up after their dogs.

The sun was warm on Sadie's face, and the shimmering blue water offered a soothing view. The day's crowd was on the quiet side, reading books or napping on beach towels while absorbing a few rays. She welcomed the calm atmosphere, which let her mind wander over recent developments while Coco sniffed her way across the sand.

Two college-aged young adults caught Coco's attention as they tossed a beach ball back and forth. Coco pulled on her leash, expressing an interest to join in. Sadie gave in to the not-so-subtle request. She unclipped Coco's leash and watched the Yorkie bound across the sand, ecstatic in her newfound freedom, sand flying up over and over as her tiny paws landed and kicked off again.

Sadie stood a distance away so as not to interfere but joined in when the others waved an invitation her way. She walked forward and caught the ball tossed by one person, then sent it on to the other. A wave of joy flowed through her. How long had it been since she'd enjoyed the simple pleasure of tossing a beach ball? It seemed like such a common activity, yet it felt as if she'd reentered her childhood. She made a mental note to add more play into her life. Whatever adult responsibilities she had—business, bills, personal commitments—there needed to be a little time to play even if only a sliver squeezed in between obligations.

Coco romped across the sand in full glory, chasing the ball as each participant passed it on to the next. After a few minutes following the triangular pattern, she settled down to watch, panting while her furry ears twitched above her head. Sadie excused herself from the game and walked over to where Coco sat, which only caused Coco to scamper off another ten feet and sit again, facing Sadie. The two repeated this pattern several times—Sadie almost catching up only to see Coco trot off again. Finally Coco tired of the game and sniffed around, plucking a seashell from the sand and presenting it to Sadie.

"We already have quite a collection, Coco," Sadie said. She bent down and gently removed the shell, placing it back in the sand. "Let's leave some shells for other visitors, okay?" She patted Coco on the head. "Let's go back to the room and get you some water."

As Sadie headed toward the hotel, Coco followed along, veering off in one direction or another along the way. On one side excursion, she returned with a cluster of seaweed, which Sadie politely declined. A different exploration brought an empty brown lunch bag, which Sadie kept, telling Coco they would take it to the hotel's recycling area.

Sadie reached the suite's patio, filled Coco's china water dish, and then took a seat on the lounge chair, knowing Coco would soon follow. Just as she expected, the Yorkie sauntered in off the sand. This time she proudly presented a wet stick, undoubtedly expecting Sadie to issue a "leave it" command. Instead, Sadie just stared. Had anyone been watching, they might have thought Sadie had gone into a trance of some sort, which wouldn't have been too far from the truth.

"You are so smart!" Sadie exclaimed, much to Coco's surprise, as well as her own. "Thank you, Coco!" Taking the stick from the petite mouth, she dropped it on the patio. She pulled Coco up into a hug, causing Coco's eyes to widen and scan the surrounding area in search of some reason for Sadie's sudden exuberance.

Sadie rushed back into the suite, deposited a confused Coco on the bed, sandy paws and all—she would be sure to leave a good tip for housekeeping—and returned to the laptop. She flipped through the still shots she'd examined before, looking for one in particular. It only took a minute to find it and confirm her suspicions.

"Aha!" she shouted.

Coco shot her a look that seemed to be more concern now than surprise. She tilted her head to one side as if waiting for an explanation. Instead, she found herself scooped up again, this time into the tote bag as Sadie raced out the door.

The appetizer hour was just getting rolling when Sadie passed through the lobby. Myrtle, who had staked out a table, waved an invitation, but Sadie simply shook her head. She stopped in the hotel's business center just long enough to print out a copy of the photo and then exited the hotel. She asked the valet parking attendant for her car and watched a text come in from Myrtle while she waited. She

sent off a quick reply just as the vehicle arrived.
Can't stay. Must see Detective Martin!

SIXTEEN

The police station wasn't far from the hotel, but it was abuzz with activity when Sadie arrived. She'd certainly picked a bad day to have a breakthrough that Detective Martin needed to hear right away. There was no right away happening in the near future, not that Sadie could tell. The entry hall was filled with people waiting to submit requests, report problems, or dispute complaints. The officer at the counter faced a line of six people juggling papers and shifting weight impatiently from one leg to the other.

"Looks like we're in for a wait, Coco." Sadie took the last remaining unoccupied seat and placed her tote on her lap. She pulled her phone out of the bag's side pocket and checked for messages. As she expected, she found a long string of texts from Myrtle.

What happened?
Are you coming back?
They have popcorn shrimp today.
Text me when you get this.
Did you get this yet?
Also half-priced wine.
What's going on?
Text me!

Sadie started to text Myrtle back but then stopped. What was she going to say? That she had a new theory that sounded too outrageous to believe? That had more potential holes in it than her favorite blue kitchen colander? She settled for something short and nonspecific.

New theory.

There, that was easy. No explanation needed.

About the murder? New information?

Sadie sighed. *Possibly.* Now she was starting to wonder herself. A mere stick on the beach had started a domino effect of thoughts that led her straight to the police station. Maybe she was putting two and two together and getting three, not four. Things weren't always what they seemed.

But sometimes they are…

Are what?

Sadie glanced at Myrtle's unexpected reply, startled. Had she really typed her thoughts into a text when she thought she was just thinking them? She was losing her mind now.

Sometimes they're complicated, she typed. *Theories, I mean. I'll explain later.* Sadie hit Send and hoped that would appease Myrtle for the time being. That and the popcorn shrimp, which was starting to sound inviting in view of the wait. Maybe she should have grabbed some before heading to the station. But then she would have gotten sidetracked talking, and this was too important. She needed to reach Detective Martin as soon as possible.

Sadie watched the line move along, eavesdropping just to pass the time. A scraggly man in his thirties was filing a report for a stolen surfboard. The officer at the counter was trying to explain that he had already filed the report three times over the past month and that there was no need to file another. The man insisted he would keep filing new reports until the surfboard was found and returned. Sadie suspected the station would be seeing the man for quite some time.

"Ms. Kramer?"

Sadie looked up, surprised to hear her name. This wasn't

a restaurant with a waitlist. No one had taken her name, so there was no reason for anyone to know she was there. Yet Detective Martin stood behind the officer at the counter, calling to her. She gathered her purse, dog, and miscellaneous items she'd brought in order to present her theory and stepped up to the counter.

"Yes, Detective," Sadie said. "How did you know I was out here?"

"I didn't," he said. "I brought paperwork out to the front desk and saw you sitting there. Can I help you with something?"

"Actually," Sadie said, leaning across the counter. "I think I can help *you*."

"How is that?" Detective Martin maintained a polite tone, but if Sadie were a betting woman, she'd put her money on patronizing as a better description.

"I have a new theory about…" Sadie lowered her voice. "…about Garrison Quinlan."

The detective's eyebrows shot up, whether out of surprise or curiosity Sadie had no idea. But she had his attention, and that was what counted.

"I brought evidence." She glanced briefly down at her purse, then back up, and then shifted her eyes from side to side, doing her best impression of a covert op. Just when she thought she had the seriously mysterious persona down pat, Coco stuck her head of the tote and yipped.

"I really don't see undercover work in your future," Martin said. He frowned as Coco leaned out of the bag and licked his wrist. "No!" he said, eyeing the Yorkie, who pulled back and returned an equally stern look. "Why don't we go back to my office, Ms. Kramer, so you can tell me what this is about. Minus the theatrics."

Sadie nudged Coco back in the tote and crossed the lobby

to a side door the detective had indicated. A buzzer beeped, and the door opened. Sadie stepped through and followed Martin down a narrow hallway. Once they were settled in a back office, Sadie pulled the sheet she'd printed at the hotel business center out of an interior pocket in her tote. Coco shuffled around at the disturbance but stayed inside, apparently not wanting to risk another run-in with Martin.

"What is this?" Martin said as he lifted the printed photo off the desk.

"A photo," Sadie said. She never could resist answering a simple question with a simple answer.

"Yes, I can see that. A photo of what, Ms. Kramer?"

Sadie drummed her fingertips on the detective's desk, impatient.

"Obviously, it's a photo taken during the filming of Garrison Quinlan's last movie."

Detective Martin nodded. "I can see that. So what?"

"So *this*," Sadie said as she unzipped a pocket and pulled out the St. Christopher medal that Coco had found on the beach.

"A common pendant," Martin said. "How is this related to Garrison Quinlan's death?"

Sadie stabbed the photo with her forefinger, dolphin bangles clattering along with the motion. "Look closely at the photo. Do you see a similar necklace?"

The detective lifted the photo and inspected it more closely. "I see someone wearing something similar, but I have no way of knowing if it's this particular pendant or not."

"Don't you have one of those computer programs that can enlarge and clarify details in photos? They have them in all the television shows."

Martin opened his mouth and closed it again, undoubtedly resisting the impulse to distinguish actual police work from that on television. "Tell you what. Just to amuse you, if nothing else, I will go have our tech department take a brief look at this through one of our television-worthy machines."

While Martin left the room with both photo and necklace in hand, Sadie stroked Coco's head, more to calm herself than for Coco's enjoyment. Had she jumped to conclusions? Was she simply wasting the detective's valuable time? She had her answer when he returned, this time with Detective Sloan in tow.

"Where did you get this pendant," Martin said, reclaiming his seat across the table from Sadie. He placed the photo and necklace, now enclosed in a plastic bag, on the table. Detective Sloan stood beside him but did not sit. He nodded a greeting of recognition.

"Coco found it."

"Coco?" Sloan asked.

As if on cue, the petite Yorkie popped out of the tote and looked at Sloan.

"Ah, I see," Sloan said. Whether or not he did was uncertain.

"Coco has a habit of fetching things," Sadie explained. "We have quite a collection of seashells and kelp on our patio at the hotel. You should see the basket of goodies we have in a basket at home—twigs, discarded Christmas ornaments, empty cereal boxes—though I suppose that's a bit off-topic."

"Indeed it is, Ms. Kramer," Martin said.

"Well, then. This St. Christopher medal was wrapped around a piece of driftwood that Coco brought in after the storm the other night. I didn't think anything of it. I'm sure people lose things on the beach all the time."

"True," Sloan said.

"But…" She reached for the necklace, only to have Detective Martin pull it back, which struck her as pointless since it was already enclosed in plastic.

"Continue," Martin prodded.

"When I started searching for photos of Garrison Quinlan online, I noticed this." She tapped the section of the photo that showed the person wearing the pendant. "This is the same one Coco found on the beach, isn't it?"

Detective Martin nodded and shrugged his shoulders at the same time, a combination of gestures that oddly resembled a tic of some sort.

Sloan spoke up this time. "We enlarged the photo and clarified the necklace. It does appear to be the same. But this is a common design, so it's impossible to know if it's the same exact one."

"I realize that," Sadie said. "But look at the photo carefully. What do you see?"

Both detectives inspected the photo, puzzled.

I'm really in the wrong business, Sadie thought to herself. *Maybe these two should run my fashion boutique and I should actually take up detective work.*

"It's obviously a filming scene," Martin said. "Cameraman and all, crew or extras on the side."

"And who's being filmed?" Sadie pointed to those in the center of the scene.

"Garrison Quinlan, obviously," Martin replied. "He's standing in front of the camera."

"And who's wearing the necklace?"

"One of the men on the side," Sloan said. He leaned closer. "Unless *that* is Mr. Quinlan. He does resemble him somewhat. Dark hair, same build."

Detective Martin shook his head. "No. Quinlan is the one in front of the camera. See the tattoo?"

"Yes," Sadie said. "Garrison Quinlan is the man standing,

being filmed. But he's not the one wearing the St. Christopher medal." She sat back and waited for the two detectives to catch up.

"So, what exactly are you saying, Ms. Kramer?" Martin asked.

Sadie leaned forward and clasped her hands. "The body that washed up on the beach is not Garrison Quinlan."

SEVENTEEN

"You should have seen their faces." Sadie dipped a popcorn shrimp in cocktail sauce and tossed it in her mouth. "Thanks for saving me some of these, by the way."

"No problem," Myrtle said. "I didn't know if you'd make it back before the end of the appetizer hour or not. Especially when you said you were at the police station."

Sadie had almost forgotten she'd sent Myrtle a quick text amid the chaos in the station's lobby.

"I don't understand," Myrtle mused. "If GQ is the one with the tattoo in the photo, then I'd think he was the body on the beach."

Sadie nodded. "That's what they thought. And it does make sense, considering the tattoo. That's how James Chalinder identified him."

"Perhaps it *was* GQ." Myrtle took a sip from a glass of wine.

"I don't think so," Sadie said. "I think it was the man sitting on the side in the photo, the one wearing the St. Christopher medal." She pulled the photo out of her purse again and set it next to the dish of cocktail sauce. She pointed to the man in question.

Myrtle frowned. "He looks a lot like GQ. That's kind of odd, don't you think?"

"Not really. He could be a stunt double," Sadie said. "Or just a fill-in actor. That's not uncommon. Stars don't always film every scene, especially those without any close-ups."

"But he doesn't have a tattoo," Myrtle pointed out, examining the photo closely. "And the way they're facing, you can clearly see the same arm on each man."

"True," Sadie said. "That part is puzzling, and it's the reason I couldn't convince the detectives my theory is correct."

"The detectives didn't keep the photo?"

"No, only the necklace. They printed a higher resolution image off the web. Apparently, their equipment is more sophisticated than the hotel's copy machine. Go figure." Sadie popped another tiny shrimp in her mouth, closed her eyes, and sighed. "Mmm, nothing better than something bread-battered and deep-fried. I'll just have to take a walk along the boardwalk to work this off." She patted one hip to emphasize her point.

"Around the area with the shops, no doubt," Myrtle said, teasing her.

"Of course," Sadie said. "You know, I've been thinking about getting one of those step-trackers to wear. Shopping would be one way to get steps in."

"Sounds reasonable to me," Myrtle said. "I could use—"

Sadie reached over and tapped Myrtle's arm midsentence. "Look over there." She pointed across the lobby, keeping her finger close to the table in order to avoid being obvious.

Myrtle followed Sadie's gesture. "That's James Chalinder leaning against the wall, isn't it? GQ's manager?"

"Yes, just outside the gift shop," Sadie said. "And Kira Fairchild is in the store. This is exactly the way I last saw them there before, acting like they don't know each other."

"Why would they do that?"

"I'm not sure." Sadie kept her eyes trained on the gift shop while reaching for another popcorn shrimp. Missing the appetizer tray, her hand dipped into the cocktail sauce instead. She pulled it back and licked the sauce off her fingers.

"I think they're just playing it cool," Myrtle said, unfazed by Sadie's behavior as if finger-licking was perfectly normal etiquette in a luxury hotel. Still, she chose to eat the next popcorn shrimp without sauce. "We know they know each other. It could be they know each other *really well*—if you get what I mean—and they don't want to broadcast it. After all, she is supposedly secretly married to GQ."

"You realize how ridiculous that sounds, right?" Sadie chuckled.

"He's the one who identified the body, right?" Myrtle said. "The news reports said GQ was identified by his manager."

"Yes, which strikes me as peculiar," Sadie said. "He worked closely with GQ, so how could he misidentify him? Unless…" She took a closer look at the picture and pointed to GQ's arm. "Unless he only looked at the tattoo."

"That could be it," Myrtle agreed. "If it's an unusual tattoo, he might not have even looked at the face. He would have felt sure just seeing the design."

"Perhaps," Sadie said. "If he was emotionally distraught, he might have rushed to a conclusion without wanting to look more carefully. I've never had to personally identify a body, but I'm sure it's disturbing. He could have misidentified him by accident."

"It's possible," Myrtle said. "But that's all the more reason to believe it really was GQ. That other man in the photo doesn't have the tattoo. What is the tattoo of anyway?" She leaned close to the photo, trying to determine the design.

Sadie shrugged her shoulders. "I can't tell. It's not clear enough in the photo, and his sleeve covers part of it anyway. But… I bet I know someone who will." She pulled her cell phone out of the tote and sent a quick text off to Amber.

Any idea what kind of tattoo GQ has?

Amber returned the text quickly. *Has? Don't you mean had?*

Of course, Sadie replied. She tilted the phone to show Myrtle and whispered, "No reason to get her hopes up. She loves him."

"Of course she loves him." Myrtle sighed. "They all love him."

What kind of tattoo did he have? Sadie typed.

Amber replied almost immediately, certainly quickly enough to show she knew the answer off the top of her head, which is what Sadie suspected.

An infinity symbol with a cactus in one side and a shark in the other.

Sadie turned the phone toward Myrtle again, who looked at the text and simply shook her head.

The text exchange with Amber ended, and Sadie set her phone down.

"Weird," Myrtle muttered. "A cactus and a shark? I've seen a lot of strange tattoos around these days, but they usually make some kind of sense."

"They make sense to the people who get them, I guess." Sadie glanced around the lobby, taking in guests with and without tattoos, and then suddenly focused her attention on the hotel's entrance. "Myrtle!" Sadie whispered. She tapped her new friend's hand and nodded toward the front door. Detectives Martin and Sloan had just entered and appeared to be heading in the direction of the gift shop.

"I wonder what that's about," Myrtle whispered back.

"Not sure, but I feel a sudden need for something to read." Sadie stood, slung her tote bag over her shoulder, and headed to the gift shop. She grabbed the first magazine she could, which turned out to be the latest issue of *People*. Ironically, the cover boasted Garrison Quinlan's handsome, smiling face. She turned her back to Kira, who was just a few yards away. She could hear two sets of footsteps approach.

"Ms. Fairchild, we'd like to ask you a few questions, preferably not here." Martin's voice was easily recognizable, though his words were spoken at a low volume. Without turning around, Sadie was quite sure the detectives recognized her. In spite of herself, she smiled. What could they do? They couldn't exactly ask her to leave.

"I've already answered your questions," Kira said. Sadie detected an odd tone in her voice that she couldn't quite place. *Annoyance? Indignation? Guilt?*

"We have a few more," Martin said. "It would be convenient if you'd accompany us willingly to the station. We can leave quietly right now."

Sadie knew the translation for that: Kira was going to the station one way or another. She might as well avoid causing a scene at the hotel. Apparently this was understood, as Kira placed a copy of *Cosmopolitan* back on the shelf and left with the detectives.

"That was interesting," Sadie said when she rejoined Myrtle.

"I saw her leave with the detectives," Myrtle said. "Are they arresting her?"

Sadie shook her head. "Didn't look like it. They just said they wanted to ask her some questions and suggested she accompany them to the police station."

"And she just went?" Myrtle quirked an eyebrow.

"Well, it was implied in their tone that she didn't have a choice," Sadie said. "I'd do the same if I were in her stilettos—a horrifying thought."

"Being questioned by the police?" Myrtle said.

"No," Sadie exclaimed, eyes wide. "Wearing stilettos!" She'd long ago switched to flats just to avoid low pumps. She reached around and rubbed her lower back, just at the thought of heels that high. Then again, she had a good thirty years on Kira, who was likely not to have Sadie's back problems. Yet, Sadie reminded herself. The years creep up on everyone. Well, maybe not on Garrison Quinlan's double, unfortunately.

"Oh my, I agree!" Myrtle said. "I have a niece who wears them, and I shudder whenever I watch her walk. I don't know how she keeps from tripping. I'd have a broken ankle within ten feet."

"This is going to make the news tonight," Sadie said.

"About the body not being GQ?"

Sadie nodded. "I think so. Either the press will get wind of it, or the police will make an official announcement." She glanced at her phone's screen, noting the time. It was already past the normal five-o'clock broadcast, but that still left the eleven-o'clock news.

"There's just one thing about this that doesn't make sense," Myrtle said.

"I know," Sadie agreed. "If Garrison Quinlan isn't the one who washed up on the beach, then where is he?"

EIGHTEEN

The late-night newscast did not disappoint. Sadie watched from the bed in her suite, green frog pajamas tucked comfortably inside the hotel's eight-hundred-thread-count sheets.

We have a new development in an ongoing story, the news anchor reported. *The police have released information saying they believe the body that washed up on the beach outside the Casa Playa hotel might not be that of well-known actor Garrison Quinlan, as originally believed. There has been no official statement about a corrected identification. There is also no word on the whereabouts of Mr. Quinlan, who did not show up for a celebrity dinner three nights ago. We will keep you posted on this developing story.*

"Well, there you have it, Coco," Sadie said, directing her comment to the Yorkie's travel palace. The petite canine lifted a sleepy head from her velvet pillow at the sound of her name. Not seeing anything of interest, she quickly curled back up and closed her eyes.

Sadie clicked the Off button on the television remote, picked up her cell phone, and debated sending a text to Myrtle. Deciding the hour was too late, she set the phone back down only to hear the double buzz of an incoming text a moment later.

I know you're awake, watching the news.

Of course, Sadie texted back to Myrtle.

So whose body do you think it is?

Sadie suspected she had the answer to that, having done an intensive web search after returning to her suite earlier. After checking references to doubles, stunt workers, fill-in extras, and a variety of other descriptions of roles a secondary person might have in relation to a star, she reached a conclusion. According to the majority of movie credits and tidbits of information, the identity of the man wearing the St. Christopher medal in the photo was likely Toby Anders, a thirty-seven-year-old from Pasadena. Several other men had worked as doubles for Garrison Quinlan over the years, and of course, they all resembled the man in the photo. But Toby Anders had been listed as GQ's double in the majority of film credits, as well as the only one during the past five films. In addition, articles indicated that Garrison and Toby had formed a friendship over the years, sometimes spending personal time together to enjoy hobbies such as fishing and golfing.

Possibly Toby Anders. Sadie sent the text with an odd feeling of dismay as if naming the man might actually make him the unfortunate victim.

Never heard of him, Myrtle sent back. *Must not be that famous.*

Worked as GQ's double for the past five years. Apparently a friend too.

There was no immediate text response from Myrtle, which Sadie understood. The information only led to more questions. Myrtle's mind was probably churning ideas just as Sadie's had been when she'd first discovered the connections. Working together, golfing together, *fishing* together? Had Toby and GQ gone out on a boat together? Was there an unexpected accident? Or an *expected* accident? Was that why

Garrison Quinlan had not shown up for the dinner? Was he a killer and on the run? Then again, maybe GQ *was* the victim? Or maybe there was no victim at all. There were too many possible scenarios.

If it was the double, then where is GQ?

Sadie had no answer for that. She was confused too. She'd posed the exact question at the police station. It made no sense that he hadn't come forward.

He would have shown up by now to say he was still alive, Myrtle continued.

I would think so, Sadie texted in return. *Coffee at nine?*

Receiving an affirmative answer, Sadie ended the conversation and set the phone aside.

"What do you think?" Sadie directed the question to Coco, who simply raised her head from her pillow. "Why wouldn't Garrison Quinlan show up as soon as he heard the news?"

Sadie slid from the bed, poked her feet into bunny slippers, and helped herself to bottled water from the suite's refrigerator. Leaving Coco—who protested with a slight whine—in the travel palace, she opened the sliding glass door and sat down at the patio table. The sound of waves building and then crashing against the shore was calming, a nice contrast to her jumbled thoughts.

As far as Sadie could figure, there were three possibilities for Garrison Quinlan's continued absence. One, he could be on the run. He and Toby could have taken a boat out together, and Toby—whether by accident or by foul play—ended up dead in the water. GQ could be hiding out if guilty of murder or afraid to come in for fear he would look guilty even if he wasn't. Admittedly, the last option was weak. In addition to that, she had yet to confirm her boat theory, though Amber's early comment about GQ's fear of water made the idea of him walking out into the ocean on his own seem unlikely.

Sadie took a drink of water and contemplated the second scenario. GQ could be unaware of the news. But how could that be? In this day and age of technology, the news was everywhere. Surely he would know. Unless he'd planned a trip away to some remote location, which would mean he'd never intended to show up at the dinner even though he was the guest of honor. That also was far-fetched. Still, Amber had pointed out a whole slew of problems he'd been facing—paparazzi, a stalker, a lawsuit, and who knows what else. Maybe he just got fed up and took off.

The third option was obvious: he was dead. Sadie had already ruled that out, at least ninety-nine percent. There was that one percent chance she was wrong, but everything she'd put together so far told her Toby Anders was the unfortunate body in the morgue, not GQ. She would try to pry that information out of Detective Martin in the morning if the police didn't make an official statement.

Yes, those were the three most likely conclusions. Garrison Quinlan was either on the run, away of his own choosing, or in the morgue. Since Sadie had ruled out the third theory, that left two viable options to pursue. Broussard would likely have some theories as well, but it was too late to text him, considering the two-hour time difference.

Stepping back inside the hotel suite, Sadie put the bottled water in the fridge and climbed into bed. Weary from analyzing, she opened the paperback mystery she'd picked up at the airport and read until she fell asleep.

NINETEEN

The ringtone of Sadie's phone barely registered, and as she emerged from sweet slumber, she was not entirely happy it had. She and Cary Grant had just boarded a jet for a Parisian vacation. Her dress was exquisite—pale yellow satin with a chiffon overlay, a designer original. She and Cary, arm in arm, were in the process of waving to his adoring fans from the doorway when the roaring of the jet engines turned into the chorus from *Fly Me to the Moon*.

"No!" Sadie muttered into her pillow. "Not the moon! Paris! Paris!" She tried desperately to cling to her dream world, but Old Blue Eyes just wouldn't let up. Multiple times her hand smacked the phone's surface, hoping to stop the interruption. On the fourth wallop or so, Sinatra's smooth crooning stopped, replaced by an annoying voice that couldn't have been more of a contrast.

"Ms. Kranger? Ms. Sally Ann Kranger?"

It took Sadie a minute to connect the name with the one she'd made up when calling the various boat rental businesses north of the hotel. *Right*, she reminded herself. *Sally Ann Kranger of the* Winnemucca Times.

"Are you there, Ms. Kranger?"

Sadie sat up and swung her legs over the side of the bed. Grasping the phone, she gathered all the pre-coffee aplomb she could and responded in what she hoped was a professional tone. "Yes, this is Sally Ann Kranger. Have you got a tip for me?" She had no idea why those particular words tumbled out, but it seemed like something a reporter might say. She looked at Coco and shrugged her shoulders.

"I think so," the voice crackled. "This is Cappy of Cappy's Coastal Cruises."

"Yes, Cappy." Sadie stood and began pacing back and forth. She shot a quick glance at the sauntering green frogs in the room's full-length mirror. Admittedly, her pajamas made for a drastic wardrobe detour from the dress she'd been wearing with Cary Grant just moments before.

"You left a message asking if we'd had a boat rental by Garrison Quinlan recently."

"Yes?" Sadie prodded. A buzz ran through her, similar to one that she'd get as a child just before opening a Christmas gift.

"Well, we didn't." The scratchy voice coughed a scratchy cough.

"Oh," Sadie said, her spirits tumbling just as quickly as they'd soared. *I left Cary Grant for nothing?*

"But I've been watching the news and I saw that his manager's name is James Chalinder," Cappy said.

"Yes, that's right." Sadie, noticing Coco now hopping impatiently from paw to paw, opened both the travel palace's latch and the suite's sliding glass door. Coco gratefully scurried outside to take care of morning business. "Go on," Sadie said.

"Well, that name sounded familiar, so I went back and checked our records." Cappy coughed again—a smoker's cough, Sadie was certain. "I found that name on a rental a few days ago."

"You did." Sadie kept a level tone to her voice, not wanting to get her hopes up.

"Yes. And we've had regular rentals under the same name

in the past, always with specific instructions."

"Specific instructions? What kind?" Sadie said, hoping for another clue.

"Nothing too unusual. He's a repeat customer, so we honor his requests." Another cough. "Well, I guess he wasn't actually the customer, now that I know the connection. Anyway, Mr. Chalinder always arranges for an ice chest of beverages. He also asks for the keys to be left on the boat so he can pick it up early in the morning. Or, apparently, so Mr. Quinlan could pick it up."

Odd, Sadie thought. "You don't worry someone will steal the boat?"

Cappy laughed and coughed at the same time. "It's not like we leave them in the ignition. We arrange a hiding place. It's not that unusual. Some fishermen like to head out early, before our office opens."

"What about returning the boat?"

"Key drop," Cappy said. "Same reason, office hours. Some boats come in late."

"So you really don't know who takes the boats out? Or when they leave? Or when they return?"

"Sure we do." Cappy's tone turned defensive. "We monitor our security footage carefully, especially at the end of the day. I check it late at night to make sure the boats are returned, wiped down, tied securely, that kind of thing. The customers know we do too."

Aha! Sadie's spirits lifted. Of course they'd have security footage. Why hadn't she thought of that before? Now she was getting somewhere. "I'd love to come by and see those tapes."

There was silence on the line. Sadie knew she was pushing the limits. She didn't really have any right to look at the footage, and he didn't need to show them to her.

"I don't know…" Cappy wheezed.

"Perhaps I could give your business more coverage. Maybe even an exclusive article, which would send more customers your way." Sadie chastised herself for the flat-out lie, justifying it at the same time. *If it helps solve GQ's disappearance…*

"Aren't you up in Nevada?" Cappy asked, confused.

Wow, lies are complicated. "No, I'm here at the Casa Playa hotel." Truth.

"Well then, come on down," Cappy said. "We're not too far up the coast from you."

* * *

Cappy's Coastal Cruises wasn't difficult to find. The ramshackle yet tidy building hugged the Pacific Ocean, as expected. Docks with wooden walkways stretched to either side, equipped with ropes, hoses, fire extinguishers, and trash cans. Several boats floated in individual slips, moored by thick rope. Cabinets of fishing tackle next to the rental office boasted rods, reels, and other fishing paraphernalia. Several open tubs marked Bait sat on the ground in front of the selection of equipment.

Cappy himself would have been easy to recognize even if he hadn't been coughing when Sadie walked in. He mirrored Popeye himself, minus the corncob pipe. And it wasn't coincidental. If the blue pants, black-and-red shirt, yellow belt, and white sailor's cap didn't prove it, the shelf of spinach cans behind the counter did. Sadie liked him immediately.

"Good to meetcha, Ms. Kranger," Cappy said, holding out a weathered hand in welcome. "And you," he added when Coco popped up to check out the surroundings.

"Likewise," Sadie said. She took a look around. "Quite an

outfit you've got going here. Looks like a lot of fun, and your boats are beautiful."

"Nothing like the seafaring life!" Cappy exclaimed. "Just look at that sparkling blue water out there. And that salt in the air is better than the finest perfume."

"I might have to take a boat out myself one of these days," Sadie said, her tone polite in spite of her differing opinion on the smell in the air. The aroma from the tubs of bait far outweighed that of the salty sea air. As perfumes went, Eau de Fish ranked far lower than her own Chanel No. 5.

"You just let me know," Cappy said. "I'll set you up on my best boat. Even give you some free bait." A big grin accompanied a wave of his arm, motioning Sadie behind the counter. She followed his direction and soon found herself in front of a small monitor that had seen better times. "I set this up while you were on your way here. This is the footage of Mr. Chalinder's boat leaving that morning."

Sadie set her tote down on the floor, leaned forward, and watched the screen closely. The black-and-white image wasn't as clear as she'd hoped, and the predawn light was dim. But a figure looking much like Garrison Quinlan—as well as Toby Anders, of course—loaded fishing tackle on the boat as well as the ice chest Cappy had mentioned in their phone conversation.

"Looks like any other fisherman loading the boat," Cappy noted. "Just an ordinary morning."

Sadie nodded. Nothing seemed out of sorts as the figure made preparations to depart. What did seem out of sorts were the tiny footsteps against the tile floor. "Coco, get back in the tote," she said, still looking at the screen. Light clicking sounds indicated the Yorkie followed Sadie's instructions.

The figure detached the boat from the dock and slowly

pulled out of the slip.

"Wait!" Sadie shouted suddenly. "Rewind a few seconds." She waited while Cappy set the footage back fifteen seconds. Again the boat began to pull away. "There! Freeze it!" She leaned even closer. "See right there?" Sadie tapped the monitor with her index finger. "There's a second figure alongside the boat."

Cappy looked at the screen. "That big guy? I think that's Bluto. He cleans the dock for me each morning and most evenings."

Bluto? Seriously? Sadie almost burst out laughing in spite of the seriousness of her discovery in the tape. She'd been a Popeye fan way back, long before Popeye's antagonist's name became Brutus. Still, Bluto or Brutus, this was not who she saw on the footage. "Forward it a couple of seconds," she said.

"There." Cappy reset the time and then leaned in. "Wait, where did he go?" He set the footage back again, and then forward. "That's odd. You're right. He was there a few seconds before, but the dock is empty when the boat pulls away."

"Exactly," Sadie said. "And there's something else missing too." She pointed to a post alongside the boat slip.

Cappy nodded. "A fire extinguisher."

"Right," Sadie said, thinking back to news reports both official and unconfirmed. *Blunt force trauma with something heavy but not sharp.*

"What does that mean?" Cappy placed his thumb and index finger around his chin and slid them down as if he might be able to pull the answer out of his stubble.

"It means it's not Bluto in the footage," Sadie said. She picked up her tote and slung it over her shoulder. "And I think I know who it is."

TWENTY

"Tell me again." Detective Martin leaned back in his desk chair and waited for Sadie to repeat the new information. "Wait. Let me get Sloan in here." He walked to the door, leaned out, called the other detective's name, and returned. Sloan soon entered and leaned against the wall beside Martin's desk.

"I saw the footage myself," Sadie said. "A second man got on that boat as it was pulling out."

"On Garrison Quinlan's boat," Martin said. He leaned back in his chair. Oddly, he sniffed, looked around, and turned back to Sadie. "Maybe it was a friend."

"Or a fishing buddy," Sloan offered.

"I can tell you're not taking me seriously," Sadie said, noting both detectives' lack of concern. "I'm telling you a second person slipped on at the last minute. It's clear in the security footage. Even the owner of the rental business agreed with me. This was not a friend or a fishing buddy. This was someone sneaking on the boat."

"The boat rented to Garrison Quinlan," Martin said.

"Though Quinlan didn't take it out," Sloan interjected.

Martin waved a hand to stop the interruption. Sadie wondered briefly if Martin was cautioning the other detective not to reveal any new details—details she obviously would be curious to know.

"Right," Sadie said, turning her gaze toward Sloan. "We

determined that last time. GQ is not the body that washed up on the beach."

Martin tapped a pen on his desktop, drawing Sadie's attention back to him. He sniffed again, and Sadie wondered if the sniffing was some sort of nervous tic she hadn't noticed on her previous visit. "We *discussed* that last time," he clarified. "We didn't specifically determine it."

"Come on, Detective," Sadie said. "I saw the police statement on the news, just like everyone else. The one you released to the press saying you suspected the body wasn't Garrison Quinlan. You must know it wasn't."

"Suspecting and knowing are two different things," Sloan pointed out. He glanced around the room as if searching for something. Sadie followed Sloan's gaze, wondering what he was looking for. Suddenly a horrifying thought struck her: she'd set her tote bag down briefly at Cappy's Coastal Cruises. It must have acquired some of the aromatic ambiance of the seaside business. Indeed, it did smell a bit fishy in Detective Martin's office. She lifted the tote off the floor and placed it on her lap, wincing as the moisture seeped into her red gingham capris.

"Yes, technically, you have a point," Sadie said, eager now to wrap up the conversation and remove her bag from the room. "And I understand that you can't share inside information with me, even though I *am* helping you." She tapped her fingernails on the desk and sent pointed looks to each detective.

The men exchanged glances. Sloan shrugged his shoulders, and Martin nodded.

"We're very grateful for your help, Ms. Kramer," Martin said. "Especially concerning the boat rental. We suspected the body might have fallen from a boat but not where that boat might have originated. Based on the rental being in

Mr. Chalinder's name, it does seem you found the correct location."

"I'm not sure fallen is the operative term for how the body ended up in the water," Sadie noted. "That sounds more like an accident than murder. And we *are* talking about murder." Both detectives remained silent, but she knew they were all in agreement.

"Hopefully, we'll know more soon," Martin said. "We'll have Mr. Cappy send the security tapes here, and we'll watch the footage."

"I think it's just Cappy," Sadie said. "He didn't look like a *Mr.* Cappy to me. In fact, he looked like…" Her voice trailed off. There was no point in pulling a cartoon character into the mix.

"Mr. Cappy or Cappy, whichever," Martin said. "In any case, we'll have a look, taking your observations into consideration."

"I think that's an excellent idea," Sadie said. She beamed, proud to be of such service to local law enforcement.

"We do appreciate your insight," Martin added. "You were at the dinner, and you saw many of the people in question, which we didn't. And you've… er… followed up on all this quite… enthusiastically."

Before Sadie could comment on Martin's hint at her overzealous involvement, Sloan made a noise that sounded like a cross between a chuckle and a gag. He topped it off with a sniffling snort.

"Are you all right?" Sadie asked. So far only focused on the case itself, she took note of Sloan's behavior for the first time, wondering if he might be getting sick or simply amused. Even worse, he could be reacting to moisture from the underside of her tote bag. She mentally kicked herself for setting the bag on the ground while at Cappy's. Tempted to move the tote off her lap again, she refrained, for fear the motion would send another wafting aroma around the room.

"Yes, I'm fine," Sloan said, clearing his throat.

"Well, I'd best be going." Sadie edged forward in her chair, preparing to stand up. "Do you have any other questions?"

Detective Martin tapped his pen on the desk again and then shook his head. "No, not at this time. Thank you for the information about the security footage. I assure you we will treat it as important."

Upon hearing the word *treat*, Sadie tried to grasp the top of her bag but wasn't quick enough. Before she could draw the sides together, Coco's head popped out, accompanied by an exponentially increased dose of Eau de Fish. To Sadie's horror, as well as that of both detectives, the petite canine hopped out of the tote and onto Martin's desk, dropping a sardine from her mouth like a benevolent Santa Yorkie. Proud of her gift, she nudged the fish forward with her nose until it reached the other side of the desk and fell into Detective Martin's lap.

"Oh my!" Sadie jumped up from her seat and gathered a rather pungent Coco into her arms. She debated an attempt to retrieve the wayward fish but thought better of it. "I'm so sorry!" she exclaimed, looking from one stunned face to the other.

"It's… all right," Detective Martin said, his tone indicating quite the opposite.

"Really, I do apologize!" Sadie said. As she placed the mischievous Yorkie firmly inside the tote, she decided it best not to mention two additional sardines she spied stuck to the interior of the bag. "Will there be anything else you need from me today?"

"Definitely not at the moment," Martin said dryly.

"Then I think this is my cue to leave," Sadie said. Hearing

no argument to the contrary from either detective, Sadie excused herself, leaving Sloan pinching his nose and Martin reaching tentatively into his lap. She raced through the precinct, earning glares from several desk officers along the way. Once outside, she reluctantly placed the pungent tote bag on the floor of the car, rolled all the windows down, and high-tailed it back to the hotel.

TWENTY-ONE

"Imagine that," Sadie said. "Housekeeping not wanting to clean that tote bag." Both Sadie and Myrtle sat on a bench next to Surf 'N Sorbet, enjoying the flavor of the day: raspberry lemon.

Myrtle nodded. "I'm sure they've seen worse."

"Certainly," Sadie agreed, though she was hard-pressed to think of what could upstage a stinky, sardine-laden tote bag. It definitely didn't fall under any of the regular categories on the guest laundry sheet. Shirts, trousers, even underwear—all accepted. But nothing on the list came close to what she'd tried to hand over to the front desk.

"Perhaps if you'd taken the sardines out first," Myrtle suggested.

Sadie dipped her spoon into a cup of sorbet and nodded. "I suppose that might have helped." She closed her eyes and sighed. This was the best flavor yet from the boardwalk kiosk.

"I doubt it helped that you set it on the front desk while guests were checking in."

"You do have a point there." Sadie had thought for a brief moment that she was about to be physically removed from the lobby.

"How did you find the groomer?" Myrtle asked. "It's a wonder they were able to take Coco in at such short notice.

"The front desk manager called them and arranged it."

Myrtle chuckled. "Probably to get you out of the hotel quickly."

"I don't doubt it," Sadie said, also laughing. "I won't get the tote back until late today."

"You're lucky the dry cleaners even took it," Myrtle said.

"Well, they weren't too thrilled about it," Sadie admitted. "And they're charging me a rush fee *and* a special handling fee."

"Still generous on their part," Myrtle said.

"Coco will be ready in a couple of hours," Sadie said. "Meanwhile… some retail therapy?"

"Why not?" Myrtle said. "We're already here on the boardwalk, and you *did* have the foresight to take a quick shower and change out of those aromatic clothes."

Finishing the sorbets, they tossed their cups in a trash can and headed for the nearest beach boutique, a strange little structure with an entrance that resembled a whale's mouth. A row of sharp teeth extended from above, while paint boasted another row on the ground.

"At least we don't have to step over teeth to go inside," Sadie murmured as they made their way through the black-and-white-molded doorway.

"Welcome to Moby Chic!" The cheerful clerk behind the counter looked to be no more than sixteen or seventeen. She wore a hibiscus-print sundress and boasted a dark tan that reminded Sadie of her high school days when slathering on baby oil and baking in the sun wasn't unusual. Most people were wiser now, and Sadie suspected the girl's tan to be sprayed on.

"I thought whales didn't have teeth," Myrtle said, looking back at the entrance.

"Some do, and some don't," the young clerk said. "There are two main categories of whales: toothed and baleen. The baleen whales, like the blue whale, for example, have more of a filtering system, while toothed whales like killer whales and beluga have teeth."

"Let me guess," Sadie said. "Not the first time you've been asked that question."

The girl laughed. "No. Maybe the hundredth. And I've only worked here a few months."

"I love your sundress," Myrtle said. "The bright colors are cheerful."

"We have them over there in several colors." The girl pointed to a rack on the wall. "There's a dressing room in the back if you'd like to try anything on."

"I just might," Sadie said. "Though I'm not sure about spaghetti straps at my, er… mature age."

"Go look," the salesgirl encouraged. "Some have wider straps."

"This one does," Myrtle called over, already looking at the selection. She held up a purple-and-fuchsia dress as Sadie approached. Inch-wide straps tied at the top in small bows. "And such a bright pattern, perfect for beachwear. Not my colors though." She handed the dress to Sadie and rummaged through the choices, picking out a bright yellow seashell print.

"We have two dressing rooms in back," the salesgirl said.

"Thank you," Myrtle said. "I'd love to try this on."

"Same here," Sadie said, holding up the dress Myrtle had passed to her. Both women headed to the rear of the store, pleased to find the dressing rooms side by side. A rustling of fabric followed as they tossed off clothing and hung it on seahorse-shaped hooks.

"Love it," Myrtle said, calling over the partition wall that separated the two rooms. "I have just the shoes for it too, gussied-up flip-flops with seashells on top."

"Really? Where did you get those?" Sadie asked, her voice muffled from having her dress only halfway over her head.

"A few shops down. We can swing by there next," Myrtle said.

"I'm in," Sadie said. "You can never have too many shoes." Even as she said the words, she thought of the overflowing shoes already in her closet at home. She'd been meaning to pack some up and drop them off at a local thrift shop for ages. Still, one more pair wouldn't hurt. *Or two, or three.*

Armed with new purchases from Moby Chic, both women headed for the boutique where Myrtle had purchased her fancy flip-flops.

"Too bad these sundresses are too casual for tonight," Myrtle said, her shopping bag dangling from her arm. "Or are they?"

"They probably are," Sadie agreed. "Though I think cast parties tend to be casual. At least more so than the dinner was the other night."

"Good," Myrtle said. "That was a crazy scene. Still, tonight should be interesting. You expect Martin and Sloan to show up, right?

"Oh, they will." Sadie laughed. "I'm certain they found the security footage Cappy sent over enlightening. In fact, I suspect Martin and Sloan will provide the main entertainment for this evening."

"And make an arrest?"

"That's my guess," Sadie said. "I already know who I'd arrest."

"My money's on GQ," Myrtle said as they entered the shoe shop. "If he's not dead, yet he's nowhere to be found, it does look suspicious." She picked up a pair of purple water shoes, inspected the rubberized sole, and wrinkled her nose. "Not too stylish."

"Agreed. But these are!" Sadie held up white flip-flops with multicolored rhinestones along the upper straps. "Look at all these sparkling colors. They'll go with everything. And they have them in black too." She grabbed a second pair. "I'm getting both."

Hearing an incoming ringtone, Sadie placed the shoes on the sales counter and fished her phone out of one pocket while pulling her wallet out of another. She stepped away from the counter. "Hello? Yes, wonderful. I'll be there shortly to pick her up." She finished the call and returned to make her purchase. She'd always thought it rude when she saw people blabbing away on their cell phones while ignoring service personnel helping them. She'd vowed never to be that discourteous.

"Coco's ready to be picked up," Sadie said after thanking the sales clerk for her help. "And the dry cleaners should be done soon too."

"I'll walk back to the hotel with you," Myrtle said.

"Nothing here you want?" Sadie said. "I can wait."

Myrtle chuckled. "The ones I told you about aren't the only pair I bought."

"Three?" Sadie guessed. "Four?"

"Six." Myrtle grinned.

"Aha!" Sadie said. "I knew we were kindred spirits from the start!"

Returning to the hotel, the women parted ways after making plans to rendezvous at the cast party later on. Myrtle wandered off to see if the spa had openings, and Sadie headed out to pick up two freshly laundered items: one petite Yorkie and one sweet-smelling tote bag.

TWENTY-TWO

The Gran Sala de las Estrellas looked especially festive, much more so than it had on the first night. Tables previously used for dining had been replaced by smaller tables located along the sides of the ballroom. An extravagant ice sculpture graced a champagne fountain in the center of the spacious salon. Tables on each side held crystal glasses waiting to be filled with the sparkling beverage. The area around it remained clear for dancing and mingling.

"They certainly went all out," Myrtle said, looking around.

"I imagine they can afford it. This movie is set to break box office records, just like his others." Sadie took in the expansive party setup, especially pleased to see a side buffet boasting miniflutes of varied chocolate confections, just the right size for… trying two or three? Possibly four? The servings were tiny, certainly not meant to be single servings. *Like tapas but with more sugar.* Instinctively she edged closer to the spread just to peruse the options: espresso mousse, mocha soufflé, crème puffs with chocolate drizzled on top, and more. It was so tempting that Sadie barely heard Myrtle calling to her.

"Sadie! What's going on?" Myrtle gestured to the center of the room where raised voices were beginning to cause a stir. Couples who'd just been dancing had stopped, some seemingly frozen in place, others backing away.

"I think we're about to find out," Sadie said. She motioned Myrtle forward, and the two women approached the center of the room. Detectives Martin and Sloan had taken places in front of the champagne fountain. Several other officers stood near exits. Martin nodded to one of the officers, who opened the door behind him.

Gasps flew through the crowd as they watched Garrison Quinlan enter. James Chalinder grasped the table of champagne flutes for support, sending a chiming sound through the ballroom as crystal glasses clinked together. He leaned forward as if he'd been punched in the stomach. Kira swayed as if about to faint but regained her composure.

Garrison crossed the floor and stopped a few yards away from Kira. "I waited for you, just like we planned," he said. "So we could be together, finally out of the spotlight. But when you didn't show up, I came back to see what happened. Imagine my surprise to find out I was dead!"

"Imagine my surprise to find out you aren't!" Kira sputtered. She shot Chalinder a dirty look.

"Of course I went straight to the police to find out what was going on," Garrison said. "They filled me in." He sent a nod toward Martin and Sloan and then turned back to Kira, his expression confused, dismayed, and angry all at the same time. "I don't understand! You were going to join me!"

"No," Chalinder said. "That's where you're wrong. She was going to go away with *me*. That was the plan all along."

To both GQ and Chalinder's surprise, Kira threw her head back and laughed. "You're both idiots. I wasn't going away with either of you!"

Sadie and Detective Martin exchanged glances, and the detective then addressed Kira. "You were going to 'take the money and run,' as they say, weren't you?"

Chalinder's face flamed red. He took an abrupt step toward Kira, but Martin restrained him. "You used me to get rid of Garrison!"

Kira shrugged her shoulders as if the plan made perfect sense to her.

"You let me think you wanted to be with me just to get him out of the way?" Chalinder continued. "Really?" He clenched his fists. "Just to get your hands on his money?"

Myrtle leaned toward Sadie and whispered, "Why do your own dirty work if you can get someone to do it for you?"

"Exactly," Sadie said.

"So you never intended to go away with me?" Garrison said as if he still couldn't believe it.

"*Or* with me?" Chalinder said. The two men exchanged a look of disbelief. For a brief moment an ironic sense of solidarity overshadowed their shock at the woman's double betrayal.

"No, boys, sorry to disappoint you," Kira said, smirking. "It's been fun, but I'm leaving you both and going away with Toby Anders."

"I don't think so," Sadie said. She turned her attention to Martin. "Isn't that right, Detective?"

"Ms. Kramer is right," Martin said. "You won't be going anywhere with Mr. Anders." He nodded to Sloan, who moved closer to Kira. "The body formerly identified as Mr. Quinlan here…" Martin extended an arm to indicate GQ.

"Very much still alive," Garrison noted.

"…has now been correctly identified as Toby Anders," Martin finished.

"What? No!" Kira's face paled, and she staggered, bumping into Sloan. She recovered quickly, giving Sloan an annoyed look before turning to Chalinder, enraged. "You imbecile! You killed the wrong guy!" She flew at him, smacking him in the chest with both hands. He stumbled backward, tripped, and fell into the champagne fountain. Sloan, who was closest to him, reached in and pulled him back out.

"How was I supposed to know that?" Chalinder shouted, shaking the bubbly off like a wet dog. "*Garrison* was supposed to be on that boat, not Toby!" His voice trailed off as he realized the inherent confession in his statement, and his eyes widened as Garrison came at him with even more force than Kira had. Once again, he landed in the fountain, and once again, Sloan pulled him out. A nearby caterer tossed him a dry towel.

"I didn't kill anyone!" Chalinder insisted as he mopped champagne off his face.

Kira turned to Garrison, tears now streaming down her cheeks. "You love fishing! Why weren't you on that boat anyway?"

"Sorry to disappoint you," Garrison said, his eyes narrowed. "I decided to leave town early to get our little *love nest* ready for us. The boat rental was already paid for, and it seemed silly to waste it, so I offered it to Toby. He loves fishing as much as I do." He shook his head and revised his wording. "Loved."

Kira shifted her gaze to Chalinder. "I don't understand. How did this get so confused? The plan seemed simple enough."

"I knew it. She was in on it," Myrtle whispered to Sadie, who just nodded.

"That's a good question," Detective Martin said. "And we were stumped at first." He turned to James Chalinder and then to GQ. "You, Mr. Chalinder, know Mr. Quinlan very well. It's hardly feasible you could mistake someone else for him."

Chalinder nodded. "Like I said, I didn't kill anyone."

"Not yourself," Martin said. "The actual killer had to be someone who could confuse Mr. Quinlan and Mr. Anders. You would have recognized Mr. Anders, so we knew it wasn't you. Thanks to Ms. Kramer here, we were able to figure out who did it, as well as how it went wrong."

"As if murder can ever go right," Myrtle interjected.

"Good point," Sadie said.

"Care to explain it for us, Ms. Kramer?" Detective Martin looked at Sadie, who nodded.

"I'll be glad to," Sadie said. She began by looking at GQ. "It took some time, but I found a private boat rental company that had sent you out on a trip that afternoon. At least they thought they had. The rental was in James Chalinder's name, but it was for you."

"He always arranged my schedule," Garrison said, shooting his manager a pointed look.

"You'd rented from Cappy's before," Sadie continued. "They always arranged to leave the keys on the boat for you and to have you drop them off through an office slot when you returned."

"Yes," Garrison said. "It was very convenient that way. I could come and go quickly, without any fuss from the annoying paparazzi."

"Exactly," Sadie continued. "Only you decided not to go, and you offered Toby Anders your place, instead. He picked up the keys on the boat, just as you always did, and planned to return them through the dropbox."

"We'd been out fishing together before," Garrison said. "Toby knew the procedure for picking up and returning the boat."

"Right, so there was no need for him to check in with anyone," Sadie said. "Which means no one knew you weren't the one who took the boat out."

"Including the killer," Martin added.

"So then who *did* kill me?" Garrison asked. In spite of the seriousness of the situation, his comment drew a few chuckles. They died down quickly. "I mean, who killed Toby, thinking it was me? And how could they get us confused? We don't… didn't… look that much alike."

"I can explain," Sadie said.

"Please," Garrison said. "I *entreat* you. Do explain."

Upon hearing a much-loved word, Coco's head popped out of the tote bag. Sadie excused herself while she pulled a small treat out of a side pocket and dropped it inside. Coco disappeared along with the treat, and Sadie looked to Martin for permission to continue. He nodded.

"When the boat rental company released the security footage, the detectives were kind enough to let me look at the tapes," Sadie said, "hoping I might recognize the second person on the boat."

"And did you?" Garrison asked. "Because clearly, it wasn't me." He spread his arms out to both sides as if confirming his physical presence.

"No, obviously, it was not you," Sadie said. "In retrospect, I can see that the man taking the boat out looked like you, but I was more interested in the second man."

"The second man?" Garrison said. "This was supposed to be a private rental." He looked at his manager, who avoided meeting his eyes.

"Yes," Sadie said. "As the boat started to pull away from the dock, a second man slipped on. He's the one that looked familiar."

"Clever," Kira said, sending an eerie look of approval to Chalinder. "You never did say how you were going to take care of things. You just said you would."

"Just like he said he'd take care of plans to cover up my escape from the public eye," Garrison said. "I never imagined this is what he had in mind, however!" He turned to Chalinder. "Don't tell me… A hitman? Is that where this is going?"

"A hitman?" Kira exclaimed. She clasped her hands together and pulled them to her chest, beaming at Chalinder. "You hired a hitman just so you could run away with me? How romantic!"

Chalinder reached up and rubbed his temples with both hands as if trying to ward off a headache.

"Continue, Ms. Kramer," Detective Martin said.

"The second man was large but nimble." Sadie remembered that had impressed her when she watched the security footage. She ran her hands over her ample hips, thinking the right exercise routine may give her the same advantage.

"Ms. Kramer?"

"Oh, yes, Detective, sorry." Sadie picked up where she'd left off. "I recognized the man but couldn't quite place him at first. Then I remembered the dinner affair—in particular, the table we sat at." She waved a hand to include Myrtle. "Three men came to sit across from us—all very rude, all very chummy and cheerful—Jack, Buddy, and Marvin. These men right here." She turned to face the three men. "The one who calls himself Buddy is the one who slipped onto the boat at the last minute."

"Jack, Buddy, and Marvin?" Garrison shouted at his manager. "That's the best you could come up with to bump me off? Those arrogant extras from the last film? Pinching pennies, I bet, as usual!" Chalinder simply shrugged, and Garrison continued. "At least you could have hired professionals. After all the money I've paid you?"

"Hey," Buddy objected. "We *are* professionals!" Marvin whipped his head around to stare at Buddy in disbelief. Jack smacked his own forehead with one hand. Martin and Sloan exchanged looks and shook their heads.

"If you were professionals, you wouldn't have killed the wrong man!" Chalinder shouted.

"He had the tattoo!" Buddy argued back. "That exact tattoo!" He pointed at Garrison's arm and then looked back at Chalinder. "Who else could have a weird tattoo like that? You told me that's how I'd know it was the right guy."

Garrison looked down at his arm and back up at Buddy. *"Weird?"* he mouthed, seemingly offended.

"Toby wasn't supposed to get that matching tattoo until next week," Chalinder said. "He needed it for fill-in scenes shooting the following week since Garrison was going to be… er… out of town."

"Wardrobe and makeup called him," Kira muttered, shaking her head. "They moved the appointment up. Some sort of scheduling conflict. You're the manager. You should have known that!"

"Okay, enough!" Detective Martin barked. He looked at Kira. "Before you wax poetic about someone hiring a hitman just so he could be with you, and before you," he said, turning his head toward Garrison, "berate Chalinder here for not paying enough to bump you off, and before you"—he turned to Chalinder—"pat yourself on the back for accidentally getting rid of the man your girlfriend *actually* planned to run away with, let's take this down to the station."

Martin and Sloan handcuffed a seething Kira and a dripping Chalinder, as well as Buddy, Jack, and Marvin. They asked Garrison to accompany them to help clarify the muddled information.

"Any chance you'll need us at the station?" Sadie asked. Detective Martin was shaking his head before Sadie even finished the question. But she was sure she saw him fight back a grin.

———

TWENTY-THREE

"Well, *that* was entertaining!" Myrtle exclaimed as she and Sadie settled into seats at the Beach Bum. A drink in the hotel bar seemed well deserved after the hoopla at the cast party, and the champagne in the ballroom was certainly out of the question.

"I thought it went quite well," Sadie mused. "A few surprises there, I must say."

A server approached and took drink orders. She placed cocktail napkins and a bowl of salty snacks on the table before walking away.

"Yes!" Myrtle said. "All that weird on-and-off behavior between that manager and Kira Fairchild? Now it makes sense. She should consider going into acting. I wonder if the prison has a drama program."

"Doubtful," Sadie said. "But you have a point. Kira had to *act* distraught over GQ's death, which she thought was real, even though she wasn't upset."

"That's why she seemed cheerful when you saw her away from the hotel."

"Exactly," Sadie said. "And then she needed Chalinder to think she was going away with him, even though she wasn't."

"Hence the subtle closeness between them that you saw on the boardwalk," Myrtle said. "But then why were they so distant in the hotel, like at the gift shop?"

"More acting," Sadie said. "Neither one wanted others to

think they were planning to go away together. That would have shown they had motive to get GQ out of the picture."

"Which they had," Myrtle pointed out.

"Yes, but not the same motive as each other. Pretty clever, actually. On Ms. Fairchild's part anyway." Sadie dropped a pretzel into her tote as their server approached and set drinks on the table. She charged both drinks to her suite against Myrtle's protests.

"You should let me pay for these," Myrtle said. "I haven't had this much fun on vacation since I witnessed a jewelry theft in Cabo one summer."

Sadie leaned forward, intrigued. "Oh, I would have loved to be in on that one! The solving of it, I mean. Not the theft itself, of course."

"It sure caused a hullabaloo around the resort," Myrtle reminisced. "They did catch the thief. It was just a setup for the insurance."

Sadie took a sip of her drink. "Well, this hotel right here offered quite the hullabaloo itself."

"Yes!" Myrtle exclaimed. "Imagine Kira planning to go away with Toby Anders all along! I didn't see that coming."

"Surprised me too," Sadie admitted. "I had a hunch she was playing both Garrison and Chalinder, but it didn't occur to me there was someone else involved."

Myrtle shook her head. "Hard enough to keep track of two men, much less three." She grabbed a pretzel from the snack mix and held it in front of her. "Can you believe we were sitting at the table that first night with three hitmen? How scary is that? Did you even suspect them, Buddy in particular?"

"No," Sadie admitted. "Not until I saw the security footage at Cappy's. But when I saw that, I remembered something that happened the first morning, when we were having coffee."

"What was that?"

"Buddy approached Chalinder across the lobby and borrowed his newspaper."

Myrtle frowned. "Everyone was looking at headlines that morning. Seems innocent enough."

"Yes, unless there's a payment hidden inside the paper for completing a job, which is what I now suspect," Sadie said. "Not so innocent then. It didn't seem like anything at the time, but Chalinder hadn't been reading, and Buddy just tucked it under his arm and joined the other two guys in the coffee line. Neither one bothered to open the paper, even knowing the victim—or thinking they did."

"That poor Toby Anders, GQ's double and friend," Myrtle said, shaking her head. "Talk about being in the wrong place at the wrong time."

"Unfortunate would be an understatement," Sadie said. "The whole thing is sort of a comedy of errors, minus the comedy part."

"Well, at least the guilty were apprehended," Myrtle said. "Amazing how many confessions flew around that room in there."

Sadie laughed in spite of the seriousness of it all. "There's nothing like anger to make people blurt things out before thinking."

A double buzz signaled an incoming text, and Sadie pulled her phone out of the tote.

Ms. Kramer.

Detective Broussard.

Sadie held the phone up to show Myrtle, and then turned it back to read the next text.

I hear there's been some activity tonight.

Must be nice to have connections, Sadie typed. "He already knows," she said to Myrtle.

"That was fast." Myrtle helped herself to another pretzel.

Precincts keep in touch with each other. Especially when worried about someone's safety.

Sadie smiled at Broussard's concern. *I was never in danger.*

"He's not going to buy that," Myrtle said, looking at Sadie's text as she sent it.

You could have been.

"Told you," Myrtle quipped as she saw Broussard's response.

Your concern is much appreciated, Sadie typed. And it was. Knowing Broussard looked out for her, even from a distance, was comforting.

I admit you did help this time, he sent back.

Really? Sadie was impressed he was willing to admit it.

You figured out the boat connection before the detectives did.

Sadie reached over her shoulder and patted herself on the back.

After about fifty phone calls, Sadie texted in return.

Sometimes that's what it takes.

This time Myrtle, still watching the texts, patted Sadie on the back herself.

Sadie finished the text exchange with Broussard, assuring him everything was fine and she'd touch base once she was back in San Francisco. She put her phone away, finished her drink in a few gulps, and set her empty glass on the table. Myrtle did the same.

"So, I guess that's it," Myrtle said as they left the hotel bar and prepared to part ways. "End of vacation, end of mystery."

"For now," Sadie said. "But not the end of a new friendship." She gave Myrtle a hug, which was enthusiastically returned. Coco's head hung over the edge of the tote bag, eyes wide at the sensation of being squished between the two women.

"Maybe we'll meet again on another trip." Myrtle released the warm embrace, and Coco's eyes visibly relaxed.

"Or even plan one together," Sadie suggested. "I'm sure we could find a little vacation mischief to get into somewhere else."

"Or mystery," Myrtle pointed out. "It seems to be in abundant supply."

"Yes." Sadie laughed. She could hardly step outside her penthouse without falling into some sort of puzzling situation. Myrtle's life clearly followed a similar path.

"Until the next adventure then," Myrtle said.

"Yes," Sadie replied. "Until the next adventure."

The Paige MacKenzie Series

Above the Bridge

When NY reporter Paige MacKenzie arrives in Jackson Hole, it's not long before her instincts tell her there's more than a basic story to be found in the popular, northwestern Wyoming mountain area. A chance encounter with attractive cowboy Jake Norris soon has Paige chasing a legend of buried treasure passed down through generations. Side- stepping a few shady characters who are also searching for the same hidden reward, she will have to decide who is trustworthy and who is not.

The Moonglow Café

The discovery of an old diary inside the wall of the historic hotel soon sends NY reporter Paige MacKenzie into the underworld of art and deception. Each of the town's residents holds a key to untangling more than one long-buried secret, from the hippie chick owner of a new age café to the mute homeless man in the town park. As the worlds of western art and sapphire mining collide, Paige finds herself juggling research, romance, and danger.

Three Silver Doves

The New Mexico resort of Agua Encantada seems a perfect destination for reporter Paige MacKenzie to combine work with well-deserved rest and relaxation. But when suspicious jewelry shows up on another guest, and the town's storyteller goes missing, Paige's R&R is soon redefined as restlessness and risk. Will an unexpected overnight trip to Tierra Roja Casino lead her to the answers she seeks, or are darker secrets lurking along the way?

Hutchins Creek Cache

When a mysterious 1920's coin is discovered behind the Hutchins Creek Railroad Museum in Colorado, Paige MacKenzie starts digging into four generations of Hutchins family history, with a little help from the Denver Mint. As legends of steam engines and coin mintage mingle, will Paige discover the true origin of the coin, or will she find herself riding the rails dangerously close to more than one long-hidden town secret?

Crazy Fox Ranch

As Paige MacKenzie returns to Jackson Hole, she has only two things on her mind: enjoy life with Wyoming's breathtaking Grand Tetons as the backdrop, and spend more time with handsome cowboy Jake Norris as he prepares to open his guest ranch. But when a stranger's odd behavior leads her to research western filming in the area—in particular, the movie *Shane*, will it simply lead to a freelance article for the *Manhattan Post*, or will it lead to a dangerous hidden secret?

The Sadie Kramer Flair Series

A Flair for Chardonnay

When flamboyant senior sleuth Sadie Kramer learns the owner of her favorite chocolate shop is in trouble, she heads for the California wine country with a tote-bagged Yorkie and a slew of questions. The fourth-generation Tremiato Winery promises answers, but not before a dead body turns up at the vintners' scheduled Harvest Festival. As Sadie juggles truffles, tips, and turmoil, she'll need to sort the grapes from the wrath in order to find the identity of the killer.

A Flair for Drama

When a former schoolmate invites Sadie Kramer to a theatre production, she jumps at the excuse to visit the Monterey Bay area for a weekend. Plenty of action is expected on stage, but when the show's leading lady turns up dead, Sadie finds herself faced with more than one drama to follow. With both cast members and production crew as potential suspects, will Sadie and her sidekick Yorkie, Coco, be able to solve the case?

A Flair for Beignets

With fabulous music, exquisite cuisine, and rich culture, how could a week in New Orleans be anything less than fantastic for Sadie Kramer and her sidekick Yorkie, Coco? And it is... until a customer at a popular patisserie drops dead face-first in a raspberry-almond tart. A competitive bakery, a newly formed friendship, and even her hotel's luxurious accommodations offer possible suspects. As Sadie sorts through a gumbo of interconnected characters, will she discover who the killer is, or will the killer discover her first?

A Flair for Truffles

Sadie Kramer's friendly offer to deliver three boxes of gourmet Valentines truffles for her neighbor's chocolate shop backfires when she arrives to find the intended recipient deceased. Even more intriguing is the fact that the elegant heart-shaped gifts were ordered by three different men. With the help of one detective and the hindrance of another, Sadie will search San Francisco for clues. But will she find out "whodunit" before the killer finds a way to stop her?

A Flair for Flip-Flops

When the body of a heartthrob celebrity washes up on the beach outside Sadie Kramer's luxury hotel suite, her fun in the sun soon turns into sleuthing with the stars. The resort's wine and appetizer gatherings, suspicious guest behavior, and casual strolls along the beach boardwalk may provide clues, but will they be enough to discover who the killer is, or will mystery and mayhem leave a Hollywood scandal unsolved?

The Moonglow Christmas Series

Mistletoe at Moonglow

The small town of Timberton, Montana, hasn't been the same since resident chef and artist, Mist, arrived, bringing a unique new age flavor to the old western town. When guests check in for the holidays, they bring along worries, fears, and broken hearts, unaware that Mist has a way of working magic in people's lives. One thing is certain: no matter how cold winter's grip is on each guest, no one leaves Timberton without a warmer heart.

Silver Bells at Moonglow

Christmas brings an eclectic gathering of visitors and locals to the Timberton Hotel each year, guaranteeing an eventful season. Add in a hint of romance, and there's more than snow in the air around the small Montana town. When the last note of Christmas carols has faded away, the soft whisper of silver bells from the front door's wreath will usher guests and townsfolk back into the world with hope for the coming year.

Gingerbread at Moonglow

The Timberton Hotel boasts an ambiance of near-magical proportions during the Christmas season. As the aromas of ginger, cinnamon, nutmeg, and molasses mix with heartfelt camaraderie and sweet romance, holiday guests share reflections on family, friendship, and life. Will decorating the outside of a gingerbread house prove easier than deciding what goes inside?

Nutcracker Sweets at Moonglow

When a nearby theatre burns down just before Christmas, cast members of *The Nutcracker* arrive at the Timberton Hotel with only a sliver of holiday joy. Camaraderie, compassion, and shared inspiration combine to help at least one hidden dream come true. As with every Christmas season, this year's guests will face the New Year with a renewed sense of hope.

Snowfall at Moonglow

As holiday guests arrive at the Timberton Hotel with hopes of a white Christmas, unseasonably warm weather hints at a less-than-wintery wonderland. But whether the snow falls or not, one thing is certain: with resident artist and chef, Mist, around, there's bound to be a little magic. No one ever leaves Timberton without renewed hope for the future.

Stand-alone: *Cranberry Bluff*

Molly Elliott's quiet life is disrupted when routine errands land her in the middle of a bank robbery. Accused and cleared of the crime, she flees both media attention and mysterious, threatening notes to run a bed and breakfast on the Northern California coast. Her new beginning is peaceful until five guests show up at the inn, each with a hidden agenda. As true motives become apparent, will Molly's past come back to haunt her, or will she finally be able to leave it behind?

For more information on Deborah Garner's books:
Facebook: https://www.facebook.com/deborahgarnerauthor
Twitter: https://twitter.com/PaigeandJake
Website: http://deborahgarner.com
Mailing list: http://bit.ly/deborahgarner

www.ingramcontent.com/pod-product-compliance
Lightning Source LLC
Chambersburg PA
CBHW021701110726
47902CB00007B/2019